One Daughter at a Time

Deb Graham

One Daughter at a Time

Other Fiction by Deb Graham

The Ghost in the Bakery
The Dim-Witted Hitman *a cruise crime*
The Cookie Cutter Legacy
Murder on Deck *a cruise novel*
Peril In Paradise *a cruise novel*

Complete list at the end of this book.
also
Don't miss the preview chapter of *Peril in Paradise!*

Chapter One

Dan, my heart is so full, there's no way I can sleep tonight, although tomorrow's a big day and I always say we need a good night's sleep before a trip. My heart keeps pounding and anxiety is coming in waves. Part of me feels like I'm leaving a part of you behind. I can't believe you're not going with us to Minnesota. What if I'm making the wrong choice? This was our first house, after all, and the girls never lived anywhere else. Your dad offered to put us up in a hotel, but I wanted to spend our last night in our house. I can't seem to make him understand we're okay financially, what with the initial insurance payout and all.

It's nearly three o'clock in the morning, and the girls are finally asleep. I wish you could see them, tumbled together on the floor like a heap of puppies. I thought we'd be done by noon and on the road, but loading the truck took longer than I expected. Yes, I can hear you saying I always underestimate how long things will take. By the time the last helper drove away, it was too late to start driving. We'll get a fresh start in the morning.

Savannah complained about taking a shower with no towels. She wasn't amused when Holly handed her the roll of paper towels from the van. We ordered take-out from Hung Hong Garden and spread out the sleeping bags on the floor. I'd left out a deck of cards and with nothing else to do in the empty house, the girls and I played games till after ten o'clock. I loved hearing their laughter. High-pitched laughter; without your booming chuckles behind it, it sounds off balance, but it made my heart happy anyway, seeing them getting along for once.

Bay kept walking around with a confused look on her baby face. "Where chair go?" "Where table go?" It's strange to think she won't remember living here. Once we settle in Glyth house, she'll think it's home. And it will be, Dan; I'm determined to make it home, even though you're not there to help me.

I miss you like crazy. Once Bay fell asleep on Lauren's shoulder, she reclined and fell asleep, too, and eventually the others joined her. And here I am, with my journal and you, sitting under the hallway lightbulb. I want to tell—

"Larkin, why aren't you asleep?"

"I can't sleep, Mom. It's spooky with the furniture all gone. The house feels like it doesn't belong to us anymore." Larkin squirmed, the dim light falling on her disheveled hair. "I've never lived anywhere else."

"How about we walk through it together one last time, Honey? Don't wake your sisters." Julie took her soft hand. "The kitchen looks so empty without the table in it, doesn't it? Wait'll you see how big our new house will be. You'll love the window seats in the kitchen. They're just perfect for curling up with a book on a rainy day."

"You keep talking about Glyth house like you know all about it, but I don't remember it at all. Can we really make it feel like home?"

"Sure, we can, you'll see. Once our stuff is arranged, you'll love it. The house is enormous, and it has lots of great places for playing hide-n-seek, and a library full of old books." Julie ran her hand over the counter, hoping her voice sounded more confident than she felt. "We made a lot of cookies here, and we'll bake more in our new home and make new memories, too. The back yard is huge. There's even a big tree you can climb. And a little stream with tadpoles in the springtime and it ices over in the winter, and there's a tall—Goodness, why are you crying?" Julie gathered Larkin into her arms.

"I miss Daddy!" she sniffed, her voice squeaking at the end. "It's not right, going off and leaving him behind. He should be here with us. Who will lift the heavy stuff? He always said that was his job."

"I miss him, too. You know he'd be here if he could; he didn't leave us on purpose. He always said we women can do anything, remember? I think he'd be proud of us." Julie smiled. "And don't worry about the heavy stuff. I told you some nice people from the church in our new town are coming to help unload the truck. It's such a small place, they're used to helping one another. It'll give us a chance to meet some new people, too. You're going to love living there."

Larkin settled into her mother's arms. "Tell me more about it."

"Well, Glyth House is old, not modern like this house. Your Great-Great Aunt Tansy always said it had its own character, from the creaky stairs to the fireplaces in every room. As I recall, the one in the front room used to blow ashes into the room when the wind blew. One time, poor Tansy got a face full when she knelt to light a fire in it." Julie chuckled. "I can still see her face. Totally covered in grey ash, with her round surprised eyes sticking out of a sheet of ash, like a mask with bright eyes."

"Uh, oh, Mom, what did she do?" Larkin giggled. "Was she mad?"

"Tansy was a good sport, and not much upset her. As I recall, she asked Old Mary, her cook, to lay the fire and she went and washed her face without another word. I wish you had known her. That woman had spunk, like you."

"If your great-aunt Tansy was here right now, what would she say?"

Julie considered. "I think she'd remind us we come from a long line of strong women, pioneers in their own right, every one of them, and she'd tell us to face the new adventure with a good heart."

"Pioneers, really? Like the ones I learned about in school, the ones with covered wagons?"

"Oh, yes, they're in our family tree. Did you know that you're a pioneer, too? Just think, we're leaving all that's familiar and heading off to make a home in a new place. That's what pioneers do."

"But I want to stay here." Tears filled her blue eyes. "I miss Daddy."

"Larkin, you know we can't do that. Great-Aunt Tansy gave us her house when she died, and new people are excited to move into this old place. Just think, they're probably awake and nervous right this minute, like we are, looking forward to moving into their new home."

"They are?" Larkin wiped her eyes on her sleeve. "I didn't think about that."

"Sure, they are. They have a son just your age. I wonder which bedroom will be his?"

"How will he know about the house?"

"What do you mean?"

"Who will tell him where to step to make sure the front door doesn't squeak if he needs to sneak in or out? He won't know about the fairy house me and Savannah made by the oak tree or about the little hole under the bathroom sink. How will he know to cut through the blackberry patch to get to the school if he's late? He won't even know what those pencil lines on the laundry room door mean."

"I almost forgot that." Julie snapped her fingers. "Come with me." They walked to the laundry room door, and Julie carefully pried off the wood trim on the left side of the doorframe. "This is where Daddy measured each of you on your birthdays, remember?

Look how little you were when you were Bay's age. We're taking this with us."

"Can you just break pieces off the house like that?"

"I think this strip of wood means more to me than it will to the new people. There's leftover trim wood in the garage." Julie offered, "Do you want to leave a note so the new boy who moves in will know about the house and the shortcuts? I have some paper in my journal."

"No." Larkin yawned. "I think he'd have more fun learning about the house, like we get to do in our new place. He's a pioneer, too."

"I think you're right. Can you sleep now?" They returned to the living room where the other girls slept, their bodies silhouetted in the streetlight's wan glow.

Dan, Larkin fell asleep as soon as she lay her head on her arm, but my mind is still racing. It feels like one of the mice in the pet store on those little wheels, running and running and not going anywhere. I want so badly to make the right decisions and I sure hoping moving is a good one. I feel bad, taking our girls from all that's familiar.

Remember that day when we sat by the river right after we found out we were expecting Lauren?

We talked about the kind of life we wanted to make for our family. We agreed we needed to live near a city for work, but once we retired or made our first million, whichever came first, we'd move somewhere rural, away from temptations and increased crime and all that. I'm trying to do that now. With Aunt Tansy leaving her house to us, it feels like this is the right time to move. Seems like every day, there's more crime and stupidity on the news and I don't want to think about all the negative influences our girls face at school. They're good, solid kids, but the reason they call it temptation is because it's...well, tempting.

I can still see your face that day when I came out of the bathroom and told you the test was positive, that we were going to be parents. Disbelief, followed by absolute joy, maybe a little wonder mixed in. I remember looking at your sparkly blue eyes and feeling like I couldn't love you more than I did at that moment.

I remember you saying you hoped it'd be a girl. "There are enough strong men in the family, both sides, but I want to raise a strong daughter." Well, you got your wish, with five girls in the family. You never got to meet little Bay, but she's as wonderful as any of her sisters.

But Dan, how can I raise them alone? How will I know what to teach them? I don't know if you can pull any strings from where you are now, but watch over us, will you?

Julie sat back as tears filled her eyes. During the day, she managed to keep up a Just Fine façade. Once the girls were asleep and no longer calling for her attention, thoughts swirled through her head like a kaleidoscope. At last, she wiped her eyes and lay her head next to Bay's on the sleeping bag. Bay reached out a sleepy hand and placed it on her mother's face.

Pioneers moved their feet and so will I.

Chapter Two

"Wake up, sleepyheads, it's time to get moving! Your grandparents will be here any minute." Julie shook each daughter awake. "We have a long drive ahead of us."

"What time is it?" Lauren groaned and rolled over. "Is it even daylight yet?"

Bay stretched and reached her arms up to Julie. "Make toast, Mama."

Larkin sat up and shook her auburn hair. "Get up, get up, you lazy sinner, we need the sheets for tablecloths and it's almost time for dinner."

As if on swivels, four faces turned to Larkin, eyes wide.

"Honey, what did you say?" Julie asked slowly.

"You know, that thing Daddy always said when he wanted us to wake up. Get up, get up, you lazy—"

"*Don't* say it again." Lauren turned to Julie. "Mom, Dad's on my mind, too. He's watching over us, isn't he?"

"Of course, silly! Heaven can't be a very big place, and where would Dad rather be than with us today? You don't think he'd go to the other end of the universe without us, do you?" Savannah swatted Lauren with her pillow. "Come on, Bay-baby, let's get you dressed while Mommy helps the bigger girls, the slugabeds."

"I'm not a slug!" Larkin howled. "You take that back!"

As Julie surveyed the tangle of bedding and sleepy girls, a car horn blared in the driveway, followed in quick order by a rap at the door.

"Good morning! Anybody awake and moving in there?"

Lauren squealed and grabbed her backpack. "Grandpa, don't come in! I'm not decent!" She bolted for the bathroom.

Holly threw open the door. *"I'm* decent, Grandpa!"

Connor set down a shopping bag and caught her in a bear hug. "Yes, my dear, you certainly are, beautiful as always, but maybe a red plaid flannel nightgown is less than ideal for the day's journey." Over her head, he winked at Julie. "Today's the day! We'll make it halfway, at least. Eighty miles from our place is still too far for running next door to borrow a cuppa, but Marsha and I are delighted to have you move a little closer to our home base. Now, tell me what I can help with first."

"Holly, Larkin, get a move on, quit throwing pillows around. Get dressed." Julie tossed Connor a sleeping bag and knelt to roll up another. "Where is Marsha?"

"Right here, lovelies, I'm right here." Dan's mother bustled in carrying stacked boxes from the local bakery. "Hot cocoa, egg sandwiches, apples, and fresh donuts, but only for ladies who are dressed and have their belongings stacked neatly by the door. Big day today."

She kissed Savannah on the head as she swept past. "Good girl, helping your sister like that. Daddy would be proud of you. Larkin, dearest, I believe the tag on your shirt goes in the back. Bay, darling, however do you look so sweet first thing in the morning? I'm going to kiss your little face as soon as you get socks on."

Julie smiled. Her mother-in-law was a force of nature, as Dan always said, and her cheerful sense of organization already had the girls moving a little faster. Before long, they sat on the floor, happily eating.

"Now, Julie, Connor and I will take turns with the driving and entertaining the little ones to start out with. With three drivers and two vehicles, we should manage quite well." Marsha wiped Bay's chin.

Julie clapped her hands. "Come on, girls, let's clean up and then we'll tell the house good-bye."

Twenty minutes later, they walked slowly through the empty house. Julie noticed a tear in Lauren's eye, but she didn't comment beyond telling them to head for the van.

She lingered in the kitchen, running her hand over the counter. *Dan, I'm leaving now. Your parents will follow me. Your dad offered several times to drive the rental truck, but I think he and your mother will be more help taking care of the girls on the trip, and I'll have Lauren with me to keep me alert. That girl can talk a blue streak, as you well know.*

I'm more worried about your folks; they forget how much energy little ones have. Connor confided he thinks Marsha has early signs of dementia, like her mother had, but I didn't notice anything different. He said it comes and goes. I sure appreciate them. In other families, I could see them stepping back, doing their own grieving. They had a major loss, too, and we all know your dad always said you were his favorite son. And he'd grin as someone gasped, until he told them you were his only son. If anything, they're closer now, eager to be involved, and they insist on helping with the girls.

I caught your mom slipping Lauren and Savannah a bit of cash for school clothes, as if she forgot the shopping trip she took them all on last month when I was at the courthouse, sorting things out. I never knew how much paperwork there could be in a liability settlement, but the attorneys assure me it'll be settled in a few months. If they need me to sign anything else, they can darn well email it to me. I wish you were here to spell me on the long drive, but we'll be fine. Connor booked us a hotel north of Chicago, more than halfway. We'll arrive at Glyth House midday tomorrow, if all goes well. I hope all goes well...there are a lot of moving parts, pardon the pun.

Tansy's neighbor, Josiah, he's the one who's been watching the place, assures me people will be ready to come help us unload the truck. Better than arriving on a weekday; I think more people will be around to lend a hand. If the girls pitch in, we should get the truck unloaded before dark. He confided they probably just want to get a look at us. A town that small, new people moving is a novelty. She paused. *I have to go.*

Goodbye, house.

Chapter Three
Two months later

Happy anniversary, darling. Eighteen years already, can you believe it? Looking at our wedding photos, neither of us looks old enough to drive, much less get married. This one picture of you and me half hidden behind the tree is my favorite. The photographer saw us holding hands between shots and he really caught the emotion of the day; outright joy, a whole lot of love and a sense of impending adventure. If we knew what lay ahead, I think we'd have held on a lot tighter.

I can still hear my mother, warning us not to get married until we finished college. "A girl has to be able to support herself and don't think about marrying a boy who hasn't proved he can finish something." How many times did I hear that?

Not saying it was easy, earning our degrees with babies in the house, but I still look at those years as being pretty wonderful. Remember the time we read the National Poverty Level chart, dreaming about what we'd do if we ever had that much money? We made our way pretty well, I'd say. And that other chart about how much it costs to raise a child to adulthood. I forget the number; well over a hundred thousand each. Clearly, they underestimated our frugality and creativity!

Of course, we've been blessed; I can't count the times somebody dropped by a box of hand-me-

downs that fit our daughters while we were in college, often right when they were outgrowing their clothes. It's funny, isn't it, how I've always shopped at second hand stores for the kids and now it's a trendy thing. Lauren points it out in all the magazines. It's called 'upcycling,' which does sound more virtuous than cheap, I admit. I caught her with the hot glue gun the other day, designing a headband for Savannah. Warms my heart to see them working together on a project and since we've moved here, they seldom beg me to take them to a store. Maybe living in a small town is helping their creativity. Who knows?

I love that cute dimple in your chin; see, it's in every wedding picture. Lauren and Holly both inherited that from you. Too bad Lauren inherited your red-headed impulsiveness, too. She's been making me doubt my mothering skills lately. I feel like I'm only one step ahead of her these days and she's picking up speed. The things she comes up with! The county school here is tougher than she expected. She's been struggling with her Aggregated Sciences class. I downloaded the textbook to see what she's studying. Brings back some memories I'd sooner forget.

Her class did blood typing last week and I had chills while she was telling me all about it after school. She tells me she might go into medicine and I believe it, the way her eyes were sparkling. I didn't tell her I borrowed my lab partner's blood when I did the same thing in college. Callie poked her finger and was already bleeding. I wasn't, so, I figured, why not? Yes, it was a problem after that miscarriage when I needed an emergency transfusion and I didn't know my own blood type, but I still remembered Callie's.

Lauren's thirst for learning reminds me of when she was on that Revolutionary War kick and kept pelting us with questions. You and I read far into the night, trying to anticipate what she'd ask next so we could answer her. Our road trip to the historical sites in Pennsylvania that summer was one of the best we had.

Remember that park ranger on the walking tour telling us that Philadelphia was the birthplace of America? Lauren blurted, "Maybe so, but I learned last summer when we were in New England that Boston was the labor room of America. And you can't make a baby without labor, or a baby country, either." The whole walking tour just stared at us like we had three heads, but I was proud of her. That's the thing with the girls; I never know if they hear a thing I say, and then they come up with a pronouncement like that.

Anyway, Dan, time for our annual recap. I like this tradition and I hope you don't mind me continuing it. Julie curled her feet under her in the big wingback chair. *Let's see. Lots of changes. I sure didn't see any of it coming a year ago. I had no idea Great-Aunt Tansy was that sick or that she'd even consider leaving her home to us. Frankly, I'm surprised she died; can't you just see her telling off the angels who came to get her? She always did things on her own terms, that's for sure. Guess I figured we'd stay in Virginia forever, but living here has been a blessing. Well, it will be, once I get my feet under me. I still wake up with panic at night, praying I'm doing the right thing.*

I put a pot of geraniums on the front porch right away. You always bought geraniums every spring, and it made the place feel a little more like home. We're adjusting to the move as well as can be expected, considering it's just been a few months. The place is huge; I'm pretty sure there are rooms we haven't even explored yet, although I bet Holly has.

She keeps me on my toes, that's for sure. Holly's been having nightmares the last few months, but I guess that's to be expected. She's only five, after all, and she's already had more upheaval than any child should have. Her big thing now is reading. Anytime we drive anywhere, she'll shout out every road sign we pass. Good thing Wilsonville is pretty small; not sure I could tolerate that driving through a big city!

I think you'd like the van I bought with some of the insurance money. I had Jack go with me to the car dealership. I guess I asked too many questions, second guessing myself. He finally said, "How do you stand up without a spine?" Hurt my feelings, but I guess he was right. I need to be the strong one now.

The financial advisor said I'm doing well after he arranged some investments and such so we're not financially strained, but it hurt writing out a check that size, even so. We had a family meeting ahead of time to talk about what kind of vehicle we wanted.

Each girl added some criteria that mattered most to her. Bay said "dink" so we made sure it had cup holders, Holly wanted big windows so we can see other cars around us, Larkin wanted a pouch in the back seat to keep art supplies in, and both Lauren and Savannah wanted a vehicle with good crash ratings.

I just wanted one big enough for everybody, yet small enough so I don't feel like I'm driving a school bus. Oh, and I hoped for a pretty color, but it seems most vans are various shades of drab. Our older girls are still jumpy passengers; I hope they'll get over that with time. The farm kids around here all learned to drive at age fourteen. Lauren and Savannah are already behind. When I suggested Lauren take driver's ed, she shook her head so hard, her headband slid off. I'm hoping they'll calm down in time. Your accident is still so fresh.

I try hard to not let the details of the accident get into the forefront of my mind, but sometimes I wake up to the sound of metal crunching and my heart stops. I hate to think of you in that horrific pile up. Seventeen cars, they said. I wonder what your last thoughts were, Dan. I hope they were of me and our daughters. I hope you weren't in pain. Did it happen in slow motion like most crises do? Was it loud? Your mom always said city people drive so bad, they give their guardian angels grey hair. I hope your angels were with you as you went toward the light. Was there really a light? Did you know, in your last moments, how much I love you? Speaking of angels, if you have any pull up there, watch over us, will you?

The reporters said twenty-six people were injured in the crash, and some were touch and go for a while in the hospital. I go over and over it in my mind. Why were you the only one who passed on? Didn't God know how much I need you, how much your daughters miss you?

I saw a poster in a gift shop. It said, "I know God won't give me more than I can handle, but sometimes I wish He didn't have such a high opinion of me." I feel like that most days. We're doing fine, we really are, but I miss you like…well, like half of my world fell off. You were my world, from the time I first saw you. Your eyelashes caught my attention. What a waste, lashes that thick and long on a boy!

She yawned. *I really need more sleep. We can talk more in the morning, okay? Well, I will talk…you haven't been holding up your end of the conversation, I must say.*

Chapter Four

Twenty minutes later, Julie perched in the window seat again. *I'm back, Dan. I can't seem to settle tonight. I'm going to regret it in the morning. I debated about letting our girls attend your memorial service. I waffled between traumatizing them and having them feel left out. Even now, when one of them has a bad day, I wonder if it's because of the memorial service. I finally decided to have a service that you would have enjoyed, not a traditional one. I remember when Annie's Lebanese grandfather died, somebody hired professional mourners to weep and wail and get people in the mood. None of that for you. I wanted it to be a celebration of you, not somber and gloomy.*

I think people were a little surprised when I told them to spread the word that anyone wearing black would not be admitted. Cheerful attire only. The girls and I all wore stripes. You always said stripes were your favorite color, no matter how many people told you stripes are not actually a color at all.

I asked Jamie to lead the service; left it all up to him. He's such a cut-up, I still don't know how he made it through divinity school. You would have loved it, Dan. He kept the whole thing really light. At one point, Jamie announced a musical number, and your mother made her way to the piano. My heart sunk, I admit; the last thing we needed was some long-winded gloomy dirge. All of your siblings went to the front and Marsha began playing.

Dan, you would have loved it. They sang that goofy song you often sang at bedtime to our daughters, the one about the frog in the lemonade, riding on the lemon slice, parasol in hand. People were so shocked, everyone burst out laughing. I don't know how your family kept straight faces, but they finished all seven verses.

Holly climbed up on the bench and hollered, "My Daddy knows that song!" when they finished, and everybody clapped. It was perfect.

After the memorial service, I had Amy hand out pens and paper and everyone wrote down some memories of you. People lingered for hours, telling Dan-stories. They laughed and it triggered the sharing of more stories. People pulled out their cell phones to record them and quite a few sent them, typed up, to me later on. One cold winter day, I'll arrange them in binders and hopefully it'll be good for the girls to read later on. You were a great dad, Dan.

I'm determined not to let the girls forget you, especially the younger ones. Sometimes when little Bay has trouble sleeping, I'll put one of your old tee-shirts on her. They come down to the floor on her, even with a makeshift belt to hold it up so she won't trip. With her little toes peeking out of the bottom, she looks like a small blonde angel. I often talk about you as I rock her to sleep, and I tell her you loved her from the day I found out she was on the way. She didn't get to meet you, but I'm hoping the stories will help her associate Daddy with feeling loved and safe.

Funny thing about those old shirts of yours. No matter how many times I wash them, they still smell like you. Fresh pine and peppermints, that's my man.

The young ones are crazy for animals now, especially Larkin. They love running and playing in the big yard, climbing the big old ash tree by the creek. They're begging for a kitten. I'm putting them off as long as I can, at least until I feel a little more settled. Larkin is so much like you, my heart hurts looking at her. She's got that same quirky eyebrow that you always raise right before you laugh.

I still think the whole universe is laughing at us. We didn't plan on five girls, did we? We talked about having two children, but after Savannah was born, we wanted one more. And we got Larkin. And then Holly was like that old song, knock, knock, knocking on heaven's door. I thought we were done having babies, but remember how urgent we both felt about having her? That girl's going places, no doubt.

Bay, our little exclamation point child, is darling. You'd enjoy her so much if you were here. She's talking up a storm now, and we finally understand most of what she says. I don't have to ask Holly to translate much anymore. Bay's favorite words seem to be "ouch," "don't," and "I do it". Oh, the perils of being the youngest! She's so sweet, I have to remind myself not to spoil her. Sometimes when I look at her eyes, I see you. Those round blue eyes are exactly like yours, and did I ever tell you how much I love you?

We talked about our future family when we were engaged, remember? We wanted to have children, as many as the Lord sent us, close together. That way, they'd be all raised, and we'd still be young enough to travel far and wide. New Zealand, China, maybe. Now it's just me and the girls and I worry about being alone when Bay is all grown up. I'm just being silly; Bay isn't even out of the high chair yet. Tansy would nod and say that's the way of the earth; people are always coming and going. I just never dreamed we wouldn't grow old together, you and me. Julie stared into the dark night and flicked away a tear.

Savannah's grown so serious these last months. I catch her watching me as if she's making sure I'm okay. She's constantly asking what she can do for me. Your leaving hit her hard, maybe hardest of all the girls. No, they all feel it in their own way. Lauren is busy finding her place in the world and the little girls are so young. Savannah even asked if she could homeschool in the fall so I won't be lonely. I'm still thinking about it, to tell the truth. Oh, with all the house needs and settling in and two of them too young for school, running out of things to do won't be a problem anytime soon, but maybe it'd be best for her.

All of them, maybe, except Lauren. She's chomping at the bit to start sophomore year. She keeps saying there's nothing lower on the social scale than a freshman, and now she'll be one of the big kids. I don't know...how much of a social scale does a town as small as Wilsonville have? I just hope Lauren will make friends. Margaret told me students come from all over the county, and the whole school is still smaller than one grade was back home.

Our old home, I mean; I keep correcting the girls when they call Virginia home. We're here to stay now, and Glyth House is our home. Funny, the house having a name instead of an address, but when anybody asks where I live, I say Glyth and they instantly know where I mean. Apparently, this place was big in society until Tansy slowed down the last few years.

There's an old album around here somewhere. I recall looking at it when my family visited Tansy years ago, a record of every event that took place here, right down to who attended and what they ate. Dances, lectures, skits and musicals, something called a salon, Sunday School picnics on the front lawn. Wouldn't it be fun to get those big summer potlucks going again? The kids would love it, and it'd be a great way to cement relationships here. Lauren keeps telling me, "Vintage is in." An old-fashioned picnic on the lawn would be a hoot.

How I wish you were here with me, Dan. Life is good, but it was more fun with you at my side. Sometimes I can almost feel you near. You're not so far away, are you?

With another yawn, Julie slipped into bed and pulled the covers up over her shoulders.

Chapter Five

Dan, I wish you were here. I wish that a thousand times a day and more so when I need to talk something out. You were always such a good listener, helped me see my way through a problem. I guess I'm just complaining, it's not a big issue; I'm just so tired all the time. I haven't slept a full night since we moved in, and it's not even the baby who's waking me up. I'd forgive Bay, she's so little, but it's Holly, night after night. I had no idea she'd have such a hard time adjusting to the move.

"Holly, I mean it, you have to sleep. At least, stay in your bed all night long like a big girl. If you can't sleep, you may look at books. You're five years old, too old to be coming in crying every night and waking me up." Julie pulled back her comforter and motioned Holly to come lie down with her. "Seriously, little one, you're too old to be carrying on like this. This is our new home. You're safe here, I keep telling you."

"But, Mommy, I'm scared. I keep hearing things and it wakes me up."

"What kind of things?"

"I don't know. People talking, people walking up and down the stairs, music, and sometimes I hear somebody whistling outside my bedroom door."

"That's just your imagination. Or maybe the wind blowing through the tree branches. There's nobody here but me and your sisters, and you're safe.

Honestly, Holly, this can't continue. You can stay here tonight, but starting tomorrow night, I expect you to be a big girl and stay in your own bed. Now go to sleep!" Julie rolled over, feeling the warmth of Holly's little - girl body against her back. Five minutes later or maybe an hour, she wasn't sure, she leaped up and grabbed her daughter. "Holly, stop screaming like that! What got into you, child?" She held Holly close, her heart thundering, matching the girl's heartbeat against her chest. "Hush, now, you're alright, it was just a bad dream."

Holly choked, "No, Mom, it was a man, a man in the doorway. He had on a tall hat and everything. And he had a mean face. He said we don't belong here."

"Stop, I mean it, it was just a dream. The doors are all locked, there's no one here but us. Stop crying, honey." She led Holly to the wide rocking chair by the fireplace. "Come sit by me until you calm down, then back to sleep you go. We have a full day tomorrow and we need to rest."

Holly snuggled beside her in the wide rocking chair. Before long, her eyes closed, but Julie's remained wide open. Holly used to be so happy, but the last few weeks, she'd barely smiled, moving through the house with wary eyes, fearful of being alone in a room. Usually, Holly was the most adaptable of the girls, but maybe the move had been more than she could handle. At her young age, she wasn't really capable of expressing deep emotion. If the nightmares kept up, Julie would have to seek help, professional help.

     A couple of weeks later, Julie dug another box out of the deep closet and thought of Dan, as had become her custom when her mind wasn't otherwise occupied.

     Dan? I hope you can hear me. Otherwise, I'm talking to myself, and that can't be good. On the other hand, at least I listen to me, which is more than I can say for your daughters.

     She shuddered at a noise, then relaxed.

     Sometimes I think I hear footsteps on the wooden staircase, but I know it's just the old house creaking. Seemed funny at first to have three staircases going upstairs, but it does make sense once Margaret told me Glyth House was used for community gatherings, dances and meetings *and such. No need for people to track mud and snow all through the house, and that door leads right to the side porch where they could shake themselves off before heading upstairs. Holly says that small room off the side entry is for hanging coats, but I don't know why she thinks that. There are no hooks or racks in there. Maybe she's right; it's a likely spot to leave off wet things on the way upstairs, I guess. The plain back staircase off the kitchen was used by servants in early days. That's what Margaret says.*

The main staircase, the one off the living room, has that wide curved banister. I'm sure you remember it. As I recall, I had to stop you from sliding down it when we visited Wilsonville the first time. I still think if you'd have hit that round knob at the bottom, we'd have only had the two daughters we already had, not the five we ended up with.

Well, Larkin discovered that round ball thing is removable. It was designed with a peg on the bottom that slips into a hole, so once it's popped off, there's nothing to stop one's flight down the banister. The first time Larkin tried it, she flew so far, she nearly hit the couch. I was painting the exterior window trim and I heard waves of giggles, never a good sign. I looked up just in time to see her flight through the window. By the time I came off the ladder, they'd arranged a heap of sleeping bags at the bottom of the banister so at least they had a softer landing. I'm not encouraging it, mind you, but I'm thinking we'll need to have fun things to do indoors once winter settles in and so long as everyone keeps their front teeth, this may not be bad.

Speaking of teeth, Holly lost her first one on Tuesday. I wondered if letting her put pretzels in her sandwich was a good idea, but what could it hurt? Turns out, it could hurt her loose tooth. Larkin teased poor Holly mercilessly about the Tooth Fairy coming. Not a good idea since she's been having nightmares. The idea of somebody in her room while she's sleeping isn't comforting. A big discussion about the current going rate broke out, which I stayed out of. Holly thought ten dollars was reasonable, Larkin said she got a dollar and a half, but Savannah said she only got three shiny quarters for each tooth she lost, and Lauren thinks Holly should pay the tooth fairy to take the nasty old tooth, who'd want that anyway? I didn't tell her I kept every one of her baby teeth to give to her when she has her own children.

Summer will be over before we know it. I don't know why summer is the fastest season, but that's what Larkin said and she's right. There's so much to do on the house before winter! I'm trying not to spend too much, but I can't do it all.

I had to have the roof replaced, and I don't want to tell you what the estimate came in at. I guess I must have gasped. All of the girls insisted they'd help, that we could do it together. Bay was so cute, lisping "I doe on woof, too." Can you just see all five of them on the peaked roof? Four stories high and all those angles; a calamity in the making, I think. I finally hired a crew from over the ridge and they'll start next week. I love the old glass in the windows, that old ripply kind, but I think we're going to wish for some modern double-pane windows when winter hits. I remember that wind rattling the windows when Tansy lived here, and I don't think I ever visited past October.

Old Josiah has been coming over most days, offering to do anything we need. Sometimes I see him out in the yard taking care of something while I'm fixing breakfast. I think he gets lonesome. Did I tell

*you how we met Josiah and Margaret in the first
place? The day our moving truck pulled up, he was out
there hammering, replacing the hinges. He said good
gates make good neighbors. It's just not like living in
the city.*

*He knows more than anybody about plants
and he's been rallying the girls to help clear the back
garden and clean up the flowerbeds. He and Margaret
even talked Savannah into pruning some stuff, once
they told her those were medicinal plants. You know
how Great-aunt Tansy was, always having just what
you need right at hand. Couldn't even mention a
headache without her concocting some poultice or
brewing herb tea. I learned very early on not to
complain about a stomach ache or she'd make me
drink chamomile tea with lavender. I still shudder,
thinking about how bad it tasted, like the soap Tansy
made. Come to think of it, that soap likely had the
same herbs in it.*

*Anyway, Josiah told Savannah a bunch of
plant names and their uses and she related it all over
dinner. I love seeing her so excited about something
outside of a book cover. She was even talking about
fixing up the old greenhouse, what Tansy called her
conservatory. I haven't seen plants in it for years, but
I'm not standing in the way of her developing new
skills. Any of them! Savannah plans to ask Josiah to
help her get it going again. He'll do it, too. I know he
misses Tansy.*

Josiah's willing to work and the girls love him. Margaret, she's his wife, said he's been at loose ends, now that their family is grown and moved away. I get chills thinking of the day when our girls have lives of their own and I won't see them on a daily basis. I appreciate Josiah's help and he sure is patient with the kids' endless chatter, but the guy is eighty-five if he's a day. I don't think his mind has any idea how old his body is these days. Being around the girls is good for him, though; they make him laugh.

The other day, Larkin came running in, saying Josiah wondered if we had thirty-eight Eileen wrenches. I tried to figure out what on earth she was talking about, but I finally had to put down my paintbrush and go talk to Josiah myself. Seems he was tightening the wheels on that wobbly red wagon she found in the shed and he needed a 3/8ths inch Allen wrench! When I corrected her, her blue eyes got all wide and innocent like they do and she said, "Josiah names all of his tools. He has screwdrivers named Philip and a plumb-Bob, and even a noisy Jack hammer. He said he needed Eileen wrenches." It was hard to keep a straight face, and old Josiah's mustache was shaking at the ends. He's a good man and we're lucky to have him and Margaret for neighbors. Oh—

Julie juggled her cell phone as she unpacked another box of dishware. "The house is a blessing, although I still can't get over how fast our other house sold and how things fell into place for us to move here so fast. Glyth House—that's what it's called— is enormous, but in pretty good shape, considering Tansy lived alone the last decade or so. I wish the girls could have seen her more often. Lauren and Savannah are the only ones who remember her. Holly was just Bay's age last time we were all here together. It always seemed too far from Ohio to Minnesota, but I admit my priorities have changed since Dan's accident. Yes, of course, I miss him like crazy."

She paused, listening. "You have to come see this place, Amy. It's like one of those old museum houses you can visit, except we live here. It's so big, I sometimes worry about losing one of the girls. If Bay wandered off and fell asleep, I might not find her at all.

"There's a huge open room on the third floor that still baffles me. Margaret, our neighbor, said it used to be a community dance hall, but I can't figure out why anybody would put that on the third floor of a home. We're not even right in town, such as it is. Still, she said her mother told her it was the happening place in her day. Lauren is already planning to invite classmates over for parties. I do hope she'll make some friends. You know how she is. Sometimes she comes across prickly, almost aloof. Shyness, I guess, but I hope kids don't discount her before she has a chance to warm up." Julie looked out the window at the girls playing in the yard.

"I guess Tansy had a lot of the rooms closed off. That's what Josiah said, that it was too much to heat the whole place, so she pretty much ignored everything but the kitchen, front room, and her bedroom with the sunny sitting room off it. Oh, and the glass room she called her conservatory. Tansy was a one for big words, even when I was a child. I'm not sure if I can afford to heat the whole thing this winter either; we may just block off the sections we actually use, maybe double up the girls in some of the bedrooms.

"Haunted? Why do you ask?" Julie rubbed her arms against a sudden chill. "I just haven't had a chance to explore the whole place yet. Margaret says there were secret passageways, and I can't imagine Tansy would have closed them off. No time now, but we'll explore it thoroughly once we settle in a bit more. The days seem to whiz past. I'm trying to focus on what really matter, but you have to admit, we've had a lot of changes in a short time. I miss everybody like crazy, but we need to make our home here now. No, we're not coming back to Virginia. I am not spineless, you take that back." Irritated, Julie said, "I gotta go. Bay is crying in the back yard."

Chapter Six

In the morning, Margaret came over and said she could use some help putting up green beans from her garden, and could Julie spare a daughter or two to help? Remembering bottling vegetables with Tansy, Julie said they'd all come over. The painting of the bathroom could wait. Margaret showed them which beans were ready for harvest, and the girls grabbed baskets. As they picked the fresh beans, Lauren taught her sisters a song she'd learned at dance camp last winter. "You gotta jump, you gotta fly, you gotta reach for the sky, you gotta…" Margaret and Julie sat on the wide porch with little Bay at their feet. The girls brought baskets of beans and the women snapped off the stem ends and dropped them into a vat of salted water.

"Hey, Larkin, you'd better slow down. We can't freeze bean stems."

"Sorry, mom, they're the same size. And I have to pick more than Lauren."

"It's not a race."

Bay toddled to her mother, pebbles in her outstretched hand.

"Yook, Mama, wocks."

"Yes, Bay, I see the rocks. They have stripes on them, see?" Julie smiled at her daughter. "Not in your mouth, honey. Rocks are not to eat."

Margaret reached for another handful of beans. "If you don't mind me asking, I've been wondering about Bay's name. I like it, mind, but I haven't heard it on a child before."

Julie chuckled. "She was named by committee vote and it's a good thing it's not worse."

"A committee? I never! How did that come about?"

Julie's gaze softened, remembering that day less than two years ago.

As another pain stabbed her swollen abdomen, Julie drew a sharp breath and grabbed the edge of the counter. Angrily, she swiped at a tear threatening to form. "Oh, no, you don't, Baby. You're not due for another five weeks. This had better not be labor."

At her routine check up yesterday afternoon, Doctor Moss had commented on her weight gain. "Up seven pounds since Friday. You didn't gain a lot with your previous pregnancies, did you?" She warned her to take it easy, and said her blood pressure was too high. "I know you have other children in the home. Are you under any other stress?"

The OB-GYN clearly wasn't up on local news; hadn't she heard about Dan's accident although it had been plastered on the front page for over a week?

Stress? You mean like burying my best friend and my reason for living, figuring out how to raise five daughters on my own, worrying about money, expecting my fifth baby? Naw, no stress, not me.

Julie had brushed her off, promising to take naps and drink more water.

"All right, but I'll need to see you again before the weekend. If your blood pressure stays this high, we may have to consider taking the baby a little early. And call me right away if you have any new symptoms. Preeclampsia can come on fast."

Hearing footsteps, Julie stood upright and pasted a smile on her face." Hi, you're back fast. Thanks for getting the mail."

"Nothing but ads. Your face is the wrong color, kinda grey, and you're sweating. You can't be sweating when it's only thirty degrees. I didn't know Virginia got this cold." Lauren studied her mother. "You alright?"

"I'm fine, just a bad headache." Julie turned the mail in her hand. "That's weird. Look how blurry this address is. I'm surprised it arrived at all."

"What are you talking about? It looks ordinary to me. Mother—" She grabbed a chair and slid it under her mother. "Mom, sit down. What's wrong?"
Julie sagged into the chair, her head reeling. "Dizzy. So dizzy…" Julie clutched her stomach and doubled over. "Hurts…"

"Savannah! Savannah, call 911. Mom's not okay!"

Savannah barreled into the kitchen, Larkin and Holly hot on her heels. "Mommy? Lauren, catch her, she's falling!"

"Help me lay her on the floor," Lauren panted.

"Her eyes look dead. She's not dead, is she?" Larkin choked, "Mommy, don't leave us!"

Savannah shouted into the phone and, within minutes, the keening wail of an ambulance broke the quiet afternoon. A young EMT questioned Lauren as the other two knelt over Julie. "Talk to me. How long as she been like this? How far along is her pregnancy? What's her urine output been? What other symptoms? Who is her doctor?"

"I…I don't know. She didn't say anything, seemed fine until I came back with the mail, then she fell over. The baby is due next month, I think." Lauren clutched Holly's hand. "I don't know anything—"

"That's okay, honey, it's going to be okay. We're going to transport your mom to the hospital, so you'd better get ahold of your dad. Is he at work?"

Holly piped up from across the room. "Our daddy lives in heaven now."

The taller EMT hissed, "Don't you remember that big accident we came up on a few weeks ago, the one out by Cliffside, with the man pinned under the semi? These are his kids. He lived here."

"And now he lives in heaven with Jesus," Holly nodded. "You won't let Mommy go with him, will you?"

The first EMT cupped Holly's face in her hand. "We'll do our best, sweetheart." She turned to Lauren. "You, is there someone you can call to stay with the children? We'll need you to come with us to answer some questions for the doctors."

"I can't leave them." Lauren froze. "I can't let Mom go alone. I don't know what to —"

"Knock it off, Lauren." Savannah snapped. "It's not your turn to have a come-apart. You go with Mom and I'll get the kids to Mrs Larson's house. She'll watch them." She shoved her sister. "Just *go*."

Lauren clung to her mother's clammy hand as the three grim-faced EMTs loaded Julie onto a gurney. "Mom? Mother, can you hear me? You go with these guys and get better, okay? Mom, don't you leave us." She scrambled into the ambulance behind the gurney, her eyes on her sisters. "Keep an eye on them, Savannah."

"We got this, Lauren."

Chapter Seven

Lauren pulled her cell phone out of her back pocket. "Hello? Oh, it's you, Grandpa. Where are you? Will you be here soon?" She wiped her face with the rough washcloth and stared, unseeing, into the mirror above the sink in her mother's room. *"Another* flight delay? Yes, I know, I saw on the news the snow is piling up in Minnesota. Please get here as fast as you can. I need…"

She hadn't slept much in the three days since her baby sister was born, and her head felt like a boulder weighing her down. Her voice cracked. "Listen, Grandpa, I'm really worried about Mom. The doctors say she's responding to the magnesium they're giving her to prevent seizures, but she still hasn't opened her eyes. She lost a lot of blood during the c-section and her blood pressure is still really really high. And she has a fever. I haven't let the girls come here yet. I don't want to scare them. No, they're okay; a neighbor is staying with them."

She listened, nodding. "I don't know. They're not telling me much, but I don't like the way their faces look when they check on Mom. Kinda solemn. They keep assuring me she's alright, but I can see the doctors are worried because she's not awake yet. I don't know what we're going to do if she—" She ran her hand down the leg of her jeans.
"I know, I know, I can't think about that now. Listen, about the baby. She doesn't have a name. No, they say

she'll be okay. She's just a little small, but she can breathe and take a bottle. They let me hold her. She has fluffy hair like a dandelion. No—I—just…Just get here as soon as you can, okay?"

Lauren broke the connection and squared her shoulders before she dialed Mrs Larsen's number. "Hello? It's me, Lauren. No, no change yet. Listen, can you bring my sisters here to the hospital? We need to decide on what to call the baby. She's three days old already and she needs a name. Yes, that's just fine. Thanks, Mrs Larsen, and thanks for…" Lauren angrily swiped at a tear. "Yes, I know everybody is praying. Thank you. See you soon."

She walked to her mother, lying still on the too-white sheets. Lauren eyed the beeping and blinking equipment warily. "Listen, Mom. I don't know if you can hear me, but try, okay? The doctors say you're going to be alright. You gotta keep fighting. We need you. I need you." She stroked Julie's hand. "Nice work, Mom. The baby is really cute. Her little hands are so tiny! The nurses told me she's the prettiest baby they've seen, but maybe they're just saying that. You're still in isolation so nobody but family can visit you.

"I'm not letting anybody see the baby, either. I told the nurses to put her little bed around the corner in the nursery, away from the big hall window. A lot of people keep coming by to check on you and they all want to see her, but it's not right that they meet her before you do. You're her mother, after all. The thing is…Listen, I decided we're going to have a family meeting and figure this out." She turned away. "I just thought you should know. If Dad was here, he'd take charge, but he's not and you're not and that leaves me. Dad always said I could do anything I set my mind to…"

Half an hour later, Lauren admonished her sisters in the hallway outside the nursery. "Listen, you guys, the baby is still pretty new, and we can't scare her. You can each hold her, but be gentle. You remember when our cat had kittens? Mom said we had to hold them and play with them, so they'd get used to being with people. I think it's the same with babies." She nodded at a waiting nurse.

"Come inside, ladies, and wash your hands over here before you hold the baby. She's going to love all of her big sisters." The nurse rolled up Holly's sleeves while Savannah scrubbed her hands. "All done? Come over here to the rocking chair. Who's going to hold her first?"

Larkin reached her arms toward the infant, but Lauren held up her hand. "No, we've all had a chance to hold a new sister except Holly. Since she's the youngest, she goes first."

The nurse arranged the baby in Holly's arms. "She's a lovely baby, just like her sisters."

"She's warm!" Holly grinned. "I love her already."

"Look at her tiny nose. How can she breathe through something that small?" Larkin tugged at the blanket. "Hand her over, I want a turn."

"Okay, okay, but you have to give her to me next," Savannah groused.

"I can see she's come into a family of strong-minded women." The nurse lifted the newborn from Holly's lap and handed her to Larkin. "Careful, now."

"Savannah, your turn to hold the baby next," Lauren said, keeping a watchful eye on Larkin. "Nurse Lucy, we need your help, please."

Told of Lauren's plan, the nurses cleared their break room table for the family to meet in and even set a box of juice at each place. "It's a big meeting, after all," Lucy smiled.

Lauren made eye contact with each of her sisters. "This is a formal meeting of the daughters of Dan and Julie McCain. We are gathered here to—"

"We all know why we're here," Savannah interrupted, "so quit being such a big shot. The new baby needs a name. We can't keep calling her The Baby. We all got to meet her, so we just need to pick a name that suits her. I think—"

"I want to call her Sunflower, Sunny for short," Larkin interrupted. "Born during a snowstorm, it'll be a good contrast."

"That's a dumb name. I'm thinking of Sandra, like that actor in those movies Mom likes," Savannah countered. "Or Catherine, the actor with the red hair."

"Those movies are sappy, and we're not naming our sister after some old actor. Rebecca is nice. What about Sharmine?" Lauren asked.

Larkin protested. "That sounds like a toilet paper commercial."

"We should call her Baby until Mommy wakes up." Holly rubbed her finger in a circle on the tabletop.

"Holly, we need to give the baby a name. We all had names before we were born." Lauren took her sister's hand. "She shouldn't have to wait." *And what if Mother never wakes up?*

"Okay, then, we're not getting anywhere arguing. Let's all write down a few names you like for her, and we'll vote," Savannah reached for a pad of paper. "Go."

"She'll need a middle name, too," Lauren said. "We'll talk about that after we come up with a first name."

Holly struggled with the pen, the tip of her tongue between her lips in concentration. Lauren and Savannah wrote quickly and tossed their folded papers in the center of the table.

"Larkin, cut it out, this is important, don't be making origami ducks at a time like this. Holly, are you done? Okay, I'll read them aloud and then we'll take a vote."

.   The girls fell silent as Lauren read the slips of paper aloud. "Annie. Penny. Sharmine. Catherine. Cassie. Angelica. Bay Leaf." Lauren scowled. "Bay Leaf? She's a little sister, not a plant, you guys."

"Keep reading," Savannah ordered. "All votes count. You know the rules."

"Another Bay Leaf, Sandra, Journey, Sunny, Bay Leaf, Sadie." She sighed heavily. "Two more for Bay Leaf. Jenny, Rebecca, Treasure, another Bay Leaf. Come on, you guys, this is serious!"

"You said we were going to vote." Holly said, "I vote for Bay Leaf. I read it on a bottle."

"You wrote all those, didn't you? No wonder you finished last," Lauren scolded. "We're not naming our baby sister Bay Leaf, and that's *final.*"

"No, it's not! We have to vote." Holly's lip stuck out stubbornly. "And Mommy always says everybody's vote is the same."

"You know, we can't name her Bay Leaf, but what about just Bay?" Savannah smiled at Holly, hoping to forestall a tantrum. "It's a good solid name, easy to say and spell, but not ordinary. Mom and Dad didn't like names from the top-ten lists."

"Bay McCain." Larkin tried it on her tongue. "I like it."

Larkin and Holly high-fived.

"There, that feels better," Lauren heaved a sigh. "Now, if Mom doesn't...you know...at least the baby has a name." She rose. "What's going on out there? Is that Grandpa's voice?"

"Where are my girls?" Grandpa's voice spilled from the hallway, followed by Grandma's higher-pitched, "Now, Gerald, remember where you are—"

The door flew open and Grandpa caught the girls in a tangle of arms and tears. "Now, now, everything's going to be all right. We'll go see your mom in a minute."
"I'm so glad you're here now!" Lauren wiped a tear.

"You've been a good big sister, rallying the troops and all." Grandma squeezed her arm. "Now, where's the new baby? I want to meet her."

"Her name is Bay, Grandpa," Holly said proudly. "I named her, and Lauren says nobody but us gets to see her until Mom wakes up."

"That's right. It's not good for everybody to meet the baby before Mother sees her." Lauren nodded.

"Bay, is it? That's a fine name," Grandpa smiled.

A nurse tapped at the door and poked her head in. "Girls, everybody, your mother is awake. Would you like to see her? Come with me."

Faces glowing, they filed down the hall. Lauren called to a nurse at the nurses' station, "Please bring our baby sister, will you? My mother is awake!"

Julie sat up, propped up by pillows as pale as her face. She smiled weakly. "Oh, my precious girls! I'm sorry I worried you, but I'm fine now. I want you to tell me everything I missed today. Marsha, Connor, what are you doing here?"

"For one thing, today is Friday, and you missed almost *four* days," Lauren corrected.

"You had a baby! The doctor pinched your tummy and the baby came out." Holly chirped, "And I named her."

"You what?" Julie shook her head in confusion. "It can't be Friday. I have a doctor appointment on Friday and…"

"Yes, it is. We were afraid you might…might not…" Savannah's voice faltered.

"Your doctor has been here every day. She delivered your new daughter." A nurse wheeled an isolette into the room. "It was touch and go for a while there, Mrs McCain. You should be proud of your daughters; they're amazing. Your eldest barely left your side. Do you want to hold your baby? Here, let's put this pillow under your arm."

Julie breathed. "I feel dazed, like Alice in Wonderland or something. Yes, let me see the baby. Dan and I didn't talk about names…I don't know what to call her."

"Call her Bay, Mommy." Larkin said. "It was Holly's idea. We had a meeting and that's what her name is."

Lauren added, "But if you don't like it—"

"Bay? It's perfect. Hello, darling Bay." Julie stroked the newborn's downy head. "She's lovely, isn't she?"

"And that's how I met Bay, not at all the way I met her sisters. But I learned that day how strong my girls were. Lauren really took charge." Julie stared across Margaret's garden. "It was a rough time. I was only seven months pregnant with Bay when Dan's accident happened. I couldn't believe he was gone, and every time I turned on the television, there was the accident scene, breaking news, playing over and over like a nightmare. I guess the stress triggered labor, although they said it was pre-eclampsia. And then the infection set in. Dan was such a help to me when the other girls were born. My heart hurt so much without him there, it was like I didn't even care anymore. Emotionally, I was a basket case, no two ways about it. Losing Dan, the funeral, a new baby on the way; too much all at once." Julie shook her head. "Not that I'm proud of it. A mother doesn't get to check out."

"You poor dear. It had to be a terrible time for you all." Margaret patted her hand. "I can just see the girls, though, holding that meeting." Margaret chuckled. "Lauren is a strong-minded young one."

Julie grinned. "You should have seen them. I woke up, foggy-minded from the fever with all four of them surrounding my bed, and Dan's parents were there, too. They said they decided it was up to them to name their little sister, since I hadn't done it yet. Holly was heart set on naming her Bay Leaf."

"Oh, my, that would have been a difficult name for a child. What is Bay's middle name? I'm figuring you stepped in about that point, am I right?"

"Her middle name is Genesis. It means 'coming into being,' and that's what happened; a new baby born, a new way of being a family moving forward." Julie straightened her back. "Lauren chose it. When I realized I'd left the naming of my baby to my little girls…Well, it was a wake-up call. I looked at my daughters' earnest little faces and pulled myself together. By the next morning, the fever was down, and I was able to go home a couple of days later."

"They're good girls, all of them. Your father-in-law was telling me when he was in your yard how proud he is of them and of you."

"Thanks, Margaret. There's really nowhere to go but onward."

Margaret nodded. "That's true. My mama used to say a body never knows how strong they are until strong's the only choice they have."

"Mine used to say don't waste the pain, that if you're going through something bad, at least learn from it." Julie sighed. "Not easy."

Chapter Eight

I wish you were here, Dan, at least to help me prioritize. You've always been so good at helping me keep my head straight amid a million interruptions. My to-do list is four pages long, not including routine things like laundry and cleaning and keeping the refrigerator full. That's no easy task, let me tell you. The little girls will eat anything dead or slow moving, but Lauren has decided she's getting fat and Savannah is as picky as ever. She reads labels on absolutely everything, as if I'm going to poison her. I guess it's helping her education…she goes and looks up every ingredient she doesn't recognize.

Margaret keeps us supplied with eggs and fresh vegetables from her garden and says she'll help us put in a garden of our own next spring. Savannah gobbles all that up. "Organic," she says. Margaret won't let me pay her for the vegetables, though. I've begun cooking more than usual a few times a week and having a couple of the girls run it over to them through the hedgerow to their house. I think they appreciate it. That old wooden gate gets a workout, let me tell you!

We're having some language challenges lately. Part of settling into a new location, I guess. Holly had a new friend over on Monday. I was in the kitchen with the window open and they were on the back stoop eating cookies. Holly explained Glyth House was where her great-great-aunt Tansy used to live. Becky said Holly made it sound fancy-schmancy, like she was putting on airs and Holly was baffled; I could hear confusion in her voice. A funny discussion ensued; if you'd been here, Dan, you and I would have been convulsed in that silent laughter like we used to do.

Becky said Tansy was a great-great ANT and Holly insisted the word is AWNT. Becky said Awnt sounded like it was British, and Holly said ants were little bugs that stole cookie crumbs like that one right there. Next thing you know, they went off to the tire swing, hand in hand.

And over dinner that same evening, Lauren said a boy at the store teased her for saying "ya'll." Said she sounded backwoods ignorant. She explained the difference between ya'll and all ya'll, the singular and plural usages, then told him anyone who thinks Uff da is a real word has no place criticizing her for telling her sisters to "all ya'll hurry it up now." The boy laughed and invited all the girls to have an ice cream cone. That's what took them so long to pick up the few things I sent them to carry. No, that word here is all of you, and I'm pretty sure Lauren is being more aware of not saying ya'll now that we live so far north. Lauren admitted she'd flown off the handle, even though she kept her voice calm. I just hope he's not in her class once school starts.

My uncle Tim and Aunt Sanna were here last month, in between starting a new mission trip in Bolivia. Sanna is so much like my mother, it's unnerving. She talks as if the conversation was a sprint and she had to get there first. Sanna's sure I'll be miserable once winter hits, insists sane people don't live in northern Minnesota during the winter. She stood there with her hands on her hips, taking in the high ceilings and wide doorways and I could see dollar signs in her mind, thinking about what it'd cost to heat the place. I doubt she's ever touched a fireplace log in her life.

Sanna said I should trade this monstrosity of a place for a decent sized house somewhere civilized and buy a summer home on the Gulf coast, or better yet, donate the money to an orphanage somewhere. My own kids are half-orphans, and I need to do what's best for them. I think Sanna is still wondering why Tansy left Glyth House to me, when she had so many other family members. I guess it'd have been clearer if Tansy had married and had kids of her own.

Sanna always seemed to brush Tansy aside, called her quirky and not in a nice way, even when I was a child. She doesn't have the memories I had from when I spent those two summers here while my mother and Dad were in Africa. Tansy taught me so many things and I guess I'm hoping our daughters will pick up some of it. Does osmosis work with houses, do you think?

Maybe Tansy left the house to me in her will because I've kept in touch all these years, writing notes and cards a few times a month.

I tell you, society doesn't value cards and handwritten notes nearly enough. After your accident, we had so many come in the mail, the mail carrier finally gave up trying to fit them in the mailbox. She just left them heaped in those official-looking plastic bins on the porch, you know, the ones the post office uses. After I threw away all the envelopes, the cards and notes filled three of those cardboard banker's boxes. They're such a comfort to read over when I miss you most. One card I really liked had a photo of a man far away on a hill overlooking a valley. The words read "Angels believe in me." We often say we believe in angels, but the idea of them believing in me, cheering me on…I needed that reminder.

The notes from the kids on the soccer team you coached are precious, written on lined paper. I wish you could see them. I heard the team mom had them all write a note about what you meant to them. She probably bribed them with extra ice cream or something. You sure made an impact in the lives of children, Dan, and not just our own. I remember my mother pressuring you to become an engineer or a doctor instead of working with children. I liked what you told her, that adults have the power to make or ruin their lives but who'll stand up for the kids? How will they develop a spine if they don't have great examples in their lives? While they were here, Sanna confided she didn't think our marriage could last when I had a law degree and you stopped at a Master's, but you were right to go into education. Some can do and others can teach, they say, but you excelled at both.

Getting tired now and I need my sleep before the kids get up at the crack of dawn. I'm still fuming over Sanna…I shouldn't let her have space in my head before bed.

She can be so critical! She thinks I'll be bored to death here with nothing to do, especially once it snows. And, of course, she mentioned again what a waste my degree is since I'm not even working in a law office. "Mentioned" being a relative term; I think she brought it up every chance she got, at least half a dozen times every day they were here, about how I could have made partner in a law firm by now if I'd only stuck with it. The only partner I ever wanted to be was yours; I knew that the first time I saw you.

Does she think our girls would be better off in some daycare or left with a sitter while I practice law fourteen hours a day, really? Or left to their own devices? Growing up, I often wished I'd had a sibling and it would have been good for Sanna, too. She has no idea how full-time raising six daughters without a single nanny or cook is. Even now, with their work at the orphanage, Uncle Tim says Sanna manages to never get her hands dirty.

I'm not exactly sitting around with my feet up eating bonbons and reading bodice-rippers. And some days I do feel like a judge and jury, arbitrating the girls' issues, so all those moot courts weren't wasted. Lauren's so bright, but her negotiating skills are nothing compared to a five-year-old Holly demanding a later bedtime. I finally compromised; Holly can stay up an hour later, but she has to stay in bed with no toys, just books. If she improves her reading, that's to the good, but so far, she's fallen asleep before the hour's up. One step ahead of them; that's all I have to stay.

Larkin's our reader; compulsive, like you. I caught her reading under her covers with a flashlight at 11 o'clock last week. I felt torn. On the one hand, you and I both encourage reading and those old Nancy Drews she found in a closet are harmless, although pretty dated. On the other hand, bedtime was at 8:30. She finally agreed to put down the book at the end of the next chapter and I went to bed. She was grumpy the next morning and the flashlight's batteries were dead. I can't scold a child for reading, can I?

I hung that great picture of you and me at the top of Mount Hood in the living room, the one where you had your arms around me and we're laughing. I don't know if it was from relief or oxygen deprivation, but we were deliriously happy we'd reached the peak, remember? Everyone who sees that photo comments on how pretty I looked, what a fine job of airbrushing my makeup just so. Makeup, my foot—my face was windburned and my eyes watered from the cold!

I found my aunt Sanna standing in front of it. She went on and on and on about how she knew from the minute she laid eyes on you how perfect we'd be together and how much she pushed for us to get married. Yeah, that's not the way I remember things, either. It felt to me like she and my mother put up as many roadblocks as they could until I told them we were going to marry regardless of their opinion and if they planned on being invited, they might want to shut up. I'm a wimp and I know it, but that was one time I stood up for myself.

I tell you, sometimes Sanna's as challenging as our daughters and has the same selective memory, too. That innocent look Lauren gets comes to mind.

Your parents have been such a help to me! Sad to say, I'm a lot more relaxed around your folks than I ever was around mine. Your dad still doesn't have much to say; I think he gave up trying to get a word in edgewise years ago. That first day they were here, he walked around and around our house, inside and out. He and Holly poked through every room, her hand in his all the way, Bay trailing behind. I think our little girl thinks he's a big toy, since he's always willing to sit on the floor at her level. How I wish you could be here, Dan. I miss listening in on your conversations with your dad. You were always so animated and now...

Chapter Nine

Later that day, Julie tucked her feet under her on the porch swing. "Margaret, I'm so glad you were able to meet Dan's folks. They're terrific, aren't they? Connor is so much like I'd imagine Dan would have been if he lived that long." She chuckled. "Connor was downright animated at lunch. He says Tansy's old furniture is worth a fortune. Authentic Period Colonial or some such. That desk in the front room is a Queen Anne, and he said it alone is worth a few thousand dollars. There's some early Amish, too. I guess I can always sell it if putting the girls through college leaves me penniless. I'm surprised; Tansy never cared about her furniture, certainly never babied it. I told him I remembered playing with my toy cars, driving them on the arms of the divan and he gasped, 'On a *William and Mary?'* as if I told him I hung the Crown Jewels as sun-catchers. Connor said it's obvious the original owners had money."

"Yes, I believe they did. There are quite a number of large homes in these parts." Margaret rubbed her arthritic hands in the sunshine.

"Connor said he wouldn't be surprised to hear there are secret passages here, as big as it is, places where servants from years ago could make their way through the house, functionally unseen. You know that's how all the old Victorian movies show them, popping up out of nowhere." Julie asked, "Do you know if that's true? I haven't really taken time to explore every inch of the place yet."

"You've had your hands full, what with the girls and unpacking and settling in." Margaret nodded. "But, yes, I know for a certain sure fact Glyth House has some of those passages you might not notice right off, and a dumbwaiter from the kitchen, too." She smiled. "Were it my house, I believe I'd keep that to myself."

"A dumbwaiter? What's that?"

"It's like a little elevator so's food could be delivered the to the third floor without anyone having to tote it. They'd put the fixings on trays and set them on shelves inside a cabinet, then someone would pull on a rope to lift it up through the shaft. At the top, they'd open a door and take it out. Handy as could be and a lot less running up and down all those steps."

Julie sat up straighter. "I like that! Do you know where it is?"

"As I recall, it's in one of those cabinets inside the butler's pantry off the kitchen. You'd think it was just an ordinary cabinet, to look at it, unless you noticed the rope and pulley to the side." Margaret smiled. "As fast as you organized your kitchen, I wonder if you didn't pile canned goods there and not know it."

"I need to make sure the girls don't find out about it." Julie chuckled. "Did I tell you about the laundry chute? I appreciate not having to haul clothes down to the laundry room, but once Bay and Holly figured it out, they've had way too much fun. I keep finding stuffed animals amongst the dirty clothes and when I scold the girls, they tell me the teddy bear wanted to ride down the slide."

Margaret laughed. "Your young ones are a caution, and I love hearing stories about their mischief. And you're a good woman to keep your sense of humor."

"It's not always easy, but they're good kids." Julie asked, "what else can you tell me about Glyth House?"

"Well, this place was built by a wealthy railroad man, one of the town's founders, name of Thomas Glyth. The stories say he was good friends with a prominent banker, George Wilson, the one Wilsonville is named after. Makes sense, that wealthy people hang out together; that's certainly true today, to my mind."

"Yes, I agree. My mother was like that, gravitating toward socialites whenever she could. My dad was different. Dad would have fit in anywhere; he had that good listener thing going for him, and he really was interested in people. Mother? Not so much; she was happiest ordering people around and doing her fund raisers. She was a decent woman, don't get me wrong, but just not a lot of warmth there. Cool as the center seed of a chilled cucumber, that was my mother for you." Julie shook herself. "Sorry, I sidetracked your story. Mom and Dad have been on my mind lately. Go on, I want to hear more local history."

"Never you mind. It must be hard, having them gone at such a young age, dear." Margaret patted Julie's hand. "The story about Wilsonville is interesting. Mysterious, some say. This area was nothing more than a logging camp in the late 1850s, far enough removed from all that led up to the Civil War, although runaway slaves were reputed to pass through here on the Underground Railroad, being so close to Canada and freedom. In fact, some say Mr Glyth, he was one of those abolitionists, might have hid slaves right in this very house."

"Really? That was brave!"

"Well, folks with a conscience find a way, don't they? Before all that, this place was made up of nothing more than a bunch of woodsmen sending trees across Lake Superior, for the most part. Oh, and an enterprising woman called Mother Martha and her pie shop. She set it up in a tent and plied the men with fresh wild berry pies. They paid her well, the story goes. That's a recipe I'd like to get my hands on."

Julie giggled. "Another brave soul, baking pies in the wilderness for some wild loggers."

"Those early settlers were strong folks." Margaret nodded. "Anyway, I was telling you about Wilson. There are rumors that Wilson and his cronies had some of the Confederate Treasury's gold spirited up here to Minnesota after President Jefferson Davis was arrested. There are some books written about it, but Tansy always pooh-poohed it. I don't know how much is true, but it makes a body wonder.

"Seems Davis was traveling with several wagons full of the gold and silver when he was arrested in Georgia, and it pretty much vanished. I'm sure some of the soldiers there pocketed some of the coins and jewelry people had donated, but it's not easy to make off with wagonloads of gold bricks unnoticed. Some of those books have a theory that it ended up being sent to Minnesota and Michigan, and a good bit of it was melted down later on."

"That makes sense, doesn't it?" Julie contributed. "Once the gold bars weren't recognizable with the Confederate States stamp on it, I guess it could go anywhere, like any other gold, or be stashed in vaults somewhere."

"Exactly. And you have to wonder how a lowly backwoods logger like Wilson could turn into a millionaire banker overnight. Where did his money come from, after all?"

"Melting gold, that's laundering money." Julie's eyes sparkled. "How much of this story is true, do you think?"

"Well, now, I'm not one for spreading tales. I don't know if any of the Confederate gold actually ended up here in Wilsonville, but I do think it's suspicious that a logger could make millions as fast as Wilson did. As your Lauren would say, it sounds sketchy. He went into banking a year after Jefferson Davis was arrested in 1865, that's a fact. Besides the town being named after him, Wilson built the bank, the high school, the library, three parks, and I heard there's a museum display all about Mr Wilson in the capitol."

"That'd be a good field trip for the girls one day, but I want to get some more boxes unpacked before we go on history jaunts. The way the girls labeled the boxes makes it hard to find which ones have necessities and which can wait. I've found ones labeled 'Green Things', 'Soft Stuff (bedroom)', 'Sand, etc', and even 'Airplane Parts'. Since when do we own any airplanes?" Julie stood. "Thanks, Margaret, this was just the break I needed. I'd better go check on the little ones. Holly and Larkin planned to explore the house this afternoon. Their tap tap tapping on walls makes it easy for me to keep track of where they are. You know how children are; so long as they're making noise, all's well. It's when they get quiet, then I worry. You and Josiah are coming over for supper, aren't you?"

"Thank you, dear, if it's not too much trouble. I'll bring a bowl of my raspberries for dessert. And some cream."

After a supper of chicken and dumplings, Julie said, "Okay, it's Lauren and Holly's turn to clean up. Soon as you're done, Margaret brought dessert and we'll have it on the porch. Come on, the rest of you, it's too nice an evening to waste indoors."

The girls played on the lawn and the adults settled into Tansy's wicker porch chairs.

"When Dan's mother and dad were here for that long weekend, Connor spent a lot of time prowling the house. Measuring, calculating, I don't know what all. He said he thinks I could open a bed and breakfast, as if we need more people in the house." Julie mused, "The times Dan and I stayed in a B & B are some of my favorite memories. There was one with a clawfoot tub and a private garden, and we enjoyed sitting out there after a long hike that day. We sipped hot cocoa in the morning and watched the deer marching through like they had a schedule to keep, and the sweet baby fawns with their mamas. I asked the owner for her recipe for stuffed French toast, and I think of Dan when I make it sometimes on Sunday mornings." She shook her head to clear it. "Anyway, what would you two think about the idea?"

"Connor's idea is a good one, if you could get some help with the chores. Maybe a woman or two from town would be willing to pitch in a couple of hours a day," Margaret said.

"Seems to be you have your hands full enough." Josiah considered. "On the other hand, he's right. After all, there's not much lodging once you get north of Grand Rapids, and Glyth House has enough bedrooms."

"At least fourteen; Connor counted." Julie shrugged. "Maybe next spring. Right now, I'm not burdened with a lot of free time, even though it'd probably bring in good money and what's another dozen people to make breakfast for? I already feel like a short-order cook some days. Connor even said he'd come in to help out during especially busy times. He's always been behind what I want to do, and I love him for it, but I suspect he's looking for a break from work. He's talking about selling the business and retiring to take care of Marsha. He said her memory is fading noticeably."

"That's too bad," Margaret sighed. "Memories are what make us human, don't you think?"

"Mommy, the kitchen is all clean and it's not my fault the floor got all wet," Holly reported.

Julie laughed, "Okay, time for dessert. Tell Lauren to bring out the small plates, please."

Chapter Ten

Dan, I wish you were here. We're settling in pretty well, but the nights are long. I'm getting used to this small-town attitude. There's not a lot of privacy; seems everybody I meet already knows everything about us, right down to the kids' names and ages. It's a far cry from the city, where we hardly even recognized people on our street. Margaret explained it's a thing here, called Minnesota Nice, like kindness and courtesy taken to a new extreme. I saw seven people pushing a stalled car out of the road last week. Back east, if a car stalled, people would drive by honking and shouting. People here do seem extra nice. The most critical thing I've heard anybody say was "That's interesting," as if they don't want to risk offending by speaking their mind.

I had a situation on Tuesday, now that I think of it. One of the moms at the playground in the town park came to me with a red face. As politely as possible, she hemmed and hawed and finally said Holly had told her little girl her sundress was sexy. She meekly said she thought it was not appropriate in a town like this, don'tcha know. I don't think it's appropriate for a child to say that in any town anywhere, do you?

I tried not to laugh as I apologized, and I talked to Holly about it once we were on our way home. She was all innocent, said what's the matter, Daddy used to say you looked sexy every time you dressed up and I did like that girl's sundress. I told her that's a word that adults use when they want to compliment a person, not children, and gave her some words she can use to tell a child she's cute in the future. We haven't lived here long. The last thing I need is people thinking my five-year-old has sex on her mind.

That "don'tcha know" is one of the phrases I'm getting used to hearing. Minnesota has its own dialect, we're learning. I asked Margaret if there was a waterfall anywhere nearby, maybe within an hour's drive or so. I thought the girls might enjoy splashing in the water on a hot summer afternoon, a change from the lake. She and Josiah nodded and said in unison, "Ransom Falls is not far, up north a piece." I asked how to get there, and Margaret pulled out her atlas and she pointed to the falls, about twenty miles due south. South, not north. I'm learning that anything worth going to is up north, and that has nothing to do with the compass direction.

"Julie. Julie?" Margaret put her hands on her hips at the base of the porch steps. "Julie, are you hearing me?"

Julie blinked, her mending still in her lap. "Oh, Margaret, you startled me! Come on up."

"It's a fine afternoon, a gift from heaven, no

question. What was you thinking about? Looked like your mind was miles away." The older woman settled into the curved wood bench beside Julie.

"Oh, the girls were digging around in the old carriage house yesterday and they found that little red sailboat, the one I learned to sail on."

"That one with the red striped sail? Always made me smile, seeing it on the lake like a piece of red ribbon candy. As I recall, you had your days of fun on that boat. I think you were the last one to use it."

"I sure did!" Julie grinned. "I spent most of two summers on that boat, zipping around the lake, playing with the sails until I figured out how to pick up speed and keep it upright."

"And now you found it. So why is your forehead creased like that?"

"My girls were so excited when we pulled it out. Savannah glommed onto it like she'd found the Holy Grail, and Larkin acts like she'll be circumnavigating the world in no time."

"In that tiny little thing? Why, it's no bigger than a thimble. What is it, about eight feet?"

"Closer to seven, just under. It'd need new sails, after all these years, but it looked seaworthy other than that. And that's the problem."

"I don't see a problem. Your girls would love being on the lake with that boat."

"They don't know how to operate a sailboat." Julie squared her slim shoulders. "I'm not letting them use the boat, and you can bet they'll have a fit when I tell them so. It's just not safe. I have to protect them."

"I'm not understanding. You're always looking for things to keep them busy. The lake is right over yonder. Once you fix up the sails, what's stopping you?"

Julie squirmed in her seat. "Kids are different these days. Living in the city, they developed different skills than I had at their ages. If it wasn't for me insisting they learn multiplication tables and spelling at home, they'd grow up relying on calculators and computer spell checkers. If I'm having a computer problem, Savannah can always figure it out, and what the little ones can do with a cell phone boggles my mind, but they can't swim."

"Is that so?" Margaret raised her eyebrow. "Lawsy, I thought every child could swim."

"Well, Lauren had lessons and Savannah, too," Lauren shrugged, "but living in the city, there was only the community pool and they were never motivated to learn. Besides, they had their dad then and he could protect them, keep them safe. Now that Dan is gone, letting them do something that dangerous is out of the question."

Margaret sat back in her seat. After a minute, she mused. "You know, some months back, I went to hear a feller give a lecture on his work in Iceland. Down to the city center in Edson, and real interesting, he was. Something he said came to mind as you were talking."

Julie listened, knowing Margaret would not be rushed. What could Iceland have to do with a red sailboat?

"He told us Iceland is a harsh place to live,

and the pictures he showed us made me believe him. It's a land where a wrong decision could cost a life and folks need skills to survive." Margaret sniffed. "Not like the namby pambies I see on the evening news. Why, one of those reporters was chasing a young man, waving his microphone and asking a question, and the young man hollered, 'I am not aware! I will not hear that subject!'" She shook her head, marveling. "It's one thing to be uneducated; no shame in that. It just means you have something to learn, but to willfully refuse to allow information to enter your mind, well, that I don't understand."

Julie redirected, "You were saying..."

"Well, I mean to say, the Good Lord gave us brains and it's our job to fill them up. With good things, mind you. The adversary puts a heap of darkness in our path and we need to sidestep it, this I know."

"Iceland. What did the speaker say about Iceland?"

Margaret harrumphed. "I did wander there, didn't I? That man, the speaker, he was saying that two fishermen drowned over seventy years ago, within a few swim-strokes of the shoreline. Iceland's a tiny place, smaller than Colorado, all told. Folks all know one another and their business, too, and the whole country mourned the sailors' passing. They made up their mind to never let that happen again. Seems there's enough ways to get kilt dead in that forbidding land, and this was one they felt they had some control over."

"I would never let my girls go there." The sailboat all but forgotten, Julie leaned forward. "What did they do?"

"They counseled together. You know, that's in their history, their very make up, since way back when the Viking ancestors gathered every spring time at the place…oh, what was it called?" She drummed her fingers on the arm of the wicker chair. "I can see the pictures in my mind clear as day, but the name escapes me. Well, whatsoever they called that place, a man whose role it was to keep their society on track recited their laws. Memorized it all, he did, like our constitution, and once a year, folks would come together to hear him shout it out. Against a tall stone wall, he read out the laws good and loud, the Law Speaker, that was his role. With the way that place was shaped, his voice carried to all those Vikings camped in that there valley. Once that was over, along and the trading and catching up like folks do, they'd settle down to solve problems that arose. Witches."

"What? Did you say *witches?*"

"Well, they had no place for anyone who's try to disrupt their ways. As I said, it was a forbidding land and folks had to work together to survive. So they'd deal with crimes and such at those meetings, then they'd counsel together to solve whatsoever problems they had. Do you know about outlaws, Julie?"

Julie's mind raced. First witches, now outlaws? "The Wild West kind?"

"No, those in our American history were just ruffians, characters without a care for what decent people worked for or needed. No, in Iceland, being outlawed was about the worst penalty a criminal could receive, short of death. In those days, a person who was a blight on society was called upon to mend his ways. Repent, like. And if he didn't, he was cast outside of society, actually out of the protection of the law, out-*lawed,* for a set period of time. In that harsh place, folks had to band together to survive. Without interaction with other humans, it was often slow death. Those who made it through their time were welcomed back into society."

"I bet they had a chance of heart." Julie brushed a leaf with her foot, making a mental note to never bring up Iceland over dinner. With her wanderlust, Savannah would likely beg to go there. No way; not a place that risky.

"I expect so." Margaret shifted. "My, how I do go on! We were talking about how they made up their mind never to have cause to grieve a drowned soul again."

"How could they prevent drowning? I know the north Atlantic waters are bitter, but Iceland is an island, with a major fishing industry. And there are lakes and rivers. Did they just forbid children to go into the water?"

"You know telling a child to keep their distance just makes things the more appealing." Margaret smiled. "Turn your back and in they go."

"Well, then, what did they do? You said they counseled…"

"Yes, and made up a rule that before a youngster could graduate from school, they had to learn to swim and swim well. Learning to swim is required in schools, right along with math and writing and it's every bit as important, maybe more so. The little ones start out in classes in the schools' indoor swimming pools, until they get good at it. Then they hold classes in lakes and eventually in the cold sea itself, so they can learn how to make their way should a wave come up."

"Really? I'm cold just thinking about it!"

"Tough people, those folks. Now, about your girls. I've seen how Savannah gets when she wants something, worrying it like hound with a meat bone, and your Larkin is not much behind. Together, they'll wear you down, this I know."

"What do you suggest I do? I have to keep them safe."

"Teach them to swim." Margaret nodded decisively. "Tell them they can't use the red sailboat until they can swim well enough to save themselves."

Julie nodded slowly. "Great idea. They can learn while we fix up the boat. With that hanging over their heads, they'll be motivated to learn to swim. And I'll relax, knowing they have that skill."

Chapter Eleven

The following afternoon, Julie dragged the little sailboat to the front yard and asked Josiah to help her lift it onto two sawhorses. She set her blue toolbox on a makeshift table, along with sandpaper, buffing compound, gel coat, and wax. On the porch, she set up her sewing machine next to a length of red-striped laminated nylon fabric. As Julie expected, the girls came running.

"Mom, can we put it in the lake after supper, can we?" Larkin jumped up and down, her face animated.

Julie didn't answer.

"Mother, do you have a pattern for the sail?" Lauren asked. "I can sew a sail if you have a pattern."

"I want to go first!" Savannah demanded. "It's not big enough for all of us."

Julie shook the can of red gel paint silently.

"Mama's not talking," Bay observed. "Mad at us?"

"No, I'm not mad at you." Julie scooped up her youngest. "I want you girls to take the sailboat seriously. It's not a toy. First—"

"*First,* it needs a new sail," Lauren said impatiently. "Is there a pattern or not?"

"I can touch up the paint, Mom," Savannah offered. "How long will it take to dry? Can we put it in the water tomorrow?"

As Julie expected, the girls protested when she told them they'd have to learn to swim before the sailboat touched water.

Larkin kicked a rock. "No fair! Savannah and Lauren already had swim lessons. And what about Holly and Bay? Are you going to leave them out just because they're young?"

Holly wailed on cue. "I want to ride in the sailboat, too! The big girls always get to—"

"Stop it right now." Julie's raised hand brooked no further argument. "You're all going to have to learn to swim. I've set up your first class for tomorrow morning. Bay can go out with me in the boat as soon as it's fixed up. You older girls will have to convince your teacher you can swim well enough to avoid drowning."

"Who's our teacher?" Lauren raised a suspicious eyebrow.

Josiah came down the porch steps. Amused, he'd been sitting on the wooden bench, listening. "That'd be me. Your mama asked me to teach you all. I can do it. I've been swimming as long as I've been walking."

"Josiah! Oh, good. This will be easy." Lauren smiled. "I was afraid she'd hired some mean old big-city swim instructor. This will be easy. You already love us."

"That I do. I value you young 'uns so much, I'll make sure and certain you can swim across the lake and back before you touch this here boat. At least out to the diving platform and back."

Savannah sagged onto the porch step. "We'll *never* get to use the sailboat. Might as well put it back in the carriage house."

"Can we go swimming now?" Holly ran down the steps in her green ruffled swimsuit. "I want to learn to swim so I can ride the sailboat first."

Julie grinned at Josiah. "Looks like your first student is ready. I didn't even see her go indoors."

Josiah took Holly's hand. "I happen to have a couple of hours free." He glanced over his shoulder with a wink. "We'll be down by the boat launch, me and Holly, should anybody want to join us."

They watched the little girl and the old man walk away.

Larkin snapped, "There's no way that pipsqueak is going to learn to swim before I do!" She bolted up the stairs, Savannah and Lauren close behind.

Julie waited with Bay on the porch until they came downstairs in their swimsuits. "Take some towels with you. Bay and I will meet you at the lake soon. And listen to Josiah."

As the girls ran down the grassy lane toward the lake, Julie and Bay walked through the gate to Margaret's porch. "Margaret, you're brilliant. The girls fell for it, and knowing them, they won't stop swimming until dark." She smiled at the older woman. "Is a picnic supper on the shore okay with you? I'll fix sandwiches and a salad, and I made some cookies, too."

"Lovely, dear. I'll bring a couple of jars of my pickles and a bag of plums."

Half an hour later, they loaded the red wagon with food and blankets to sit on. "You two are such a blessing," Julie said as they walked to the lake.

"You're good friends to me and like extra grandparents to my daughters. I really think God put you and Josiah in our lives, and I'm grateful."

"No, it's the other way around," Margaret demurred. "Your family is keeping us young." She pointed to the beach where Josiah stood waist-deep with the girls. "You know, dear, I'd enjoy a turn in the sailboat, too."

"Fine by me," Julie smiled. "You can swim, right?"

Chapter Twelve

Julie stumbled up the stairs, peeked into each bedroom at her sleeping daughters, then closed her bedroom door. She yawned and slipped into her pajamas. She sat on the end of her bed, muttering to herself. "No, I'm behind in my journaling. I can't keep putting it off. Just a few lines. Then sleep."

She reached for her hardbound book and was soon engrossed in writing, her fatigue pushed aside.

I keep hoping I'm making the right decisions along the way. There's so much to do, but I'm trying to build in time with each girl daily. Josiah helped build a fire ring out of bricks behind the carriage house and we've been spending most evenings out there. We agree those fudgy cookies make the best s'mores, but the girls have been really creative coming up with things we can toast on the end of a stick. Caramel was good and I liked the taffy, but gummy fruit wedges were awful. They melted so fast and we had streams of molten sugary lava everywhere. What a mess.

And we haven't perfected foil dinners yet, but the attempts have been pretty creative. Northern pike and asparagus was good, although pike have those bones at every angle, and it was hard for the little ones to eat. I had to pick apart the fish for Bay; it was like baby food all over again. How do pike swim when their bones are all out of order like that?

She yawned. *I showed Savannah how to roast potatoes, apples, and eggs in the coals and you'd have thought I invented fire itself, she was that impressed. Dan always said it's good for the girls to be awed every so often. Savannah has a real knack for cooking. I made a chart for them to help with dinner. It's called supper here, and whatever it is, I need help. And it's good for them to learn life-skills.*

Lauren, Savannah, and Larkin are so competitive, they even try to outdo one another with dinner. Savannah pores over cookbooks, lamenting— loudly—the lack of a big-city grocery store nearby where she could get fancy ingredients. I keep telling her how lucky she is to have access to only wholesome foods instead of over-processed stuff. She visited Margaret last week and ended up helping her cut back some overgrown blackberry canes.

She came back wide-eyed. "Did you know Margaret and Josiah have an organic garden?"

Well, yeah, like the whole world until fairly recently!

She turned off the bedside lamp and knelt to pray. Rising, she rolled under the covers. As usual, once her mind was still, Dan filled her thoughts.

I'm trying so hard to raise the girls well. Like you said, they need to know what real love feels like so when they encounter counterfeits later on, they'll know the difference. I hope they find husbands as great as you were, Dan. For now, I'm concentrating on making memories with them. She fluffed her pillow. *I can't believe how fast they're all growing. Larkin likes to measure herself against my height, back to back. She still has a few inches to grow, but it's not for lack of trying. Summer's great in Minnesota, except the mosquitos are the size of bumblebees and vicious. Everybody in town says the winters here are nothing to fool around with.*

I'm afraid once school starts, there won't be enough time for family things. I'm trying to cram in as much as I can. We're going camping again on Friday. Okay, just down by the creek at the far end of the property, but if we have a fire and sleep in a tent, it counts, right? I wish you could go with us. The girls are so much fun, even amid their bickering, which is pretty much nonstop some days.

I wish you could help me, Dan. Sometimes I don't know what to say to the girls, and you were a better listener, too. I worry that I won't be able to teach them all they need to know. Lauren's at a risky time of life. You and I weren't much older than that when we met, although we were certainly years more mature. Now, I can hear you chuckling, and you're wrong. I was not boy crazy! I wasn't. I just knew what I wanted, and you fit the picture perfectly. I worry that I won't be able to teach them all they need to know. I mean look how fast they're growing!

Well, Dan, it's late and—

An hour later, Julie leaped out of bed, knocking the lamp off the table before her feet hit the floor.

Holly's screams echoed down the hallway. Julie ran to her room, colliding with Lauren in the doorway.

"Mother, is it another nightmare?"

"I sure hope so. It's either that or she's being eaten alive by a dragon." Julie rushed to Holly's bed.

Holly sat up, the bed covers to her neck, her eyes the size of golf balls. "Mommy, the man said— He said—" she whimpered.

Julie looked at the corner where Holly pointed. "Honey, calm down, you're safe, Mommy's here."

"What man?" Lauren asked. "What did he say?"

"The old man with the walking stick. He said this is his house, not ours." Holly sniffed and wiped her nose on Julie's pajama top. "Then the grandma lady in the long dress came and made him go away. I didn't like him."

"You're safe, Holly, don't cry." Julie rocked her in her arms. "Lauren, go back to bed. I'll sit with her a while."

"There are strangers in our house, or my sister is seeing things, and I'm supposed to go to bed like nothing happened?"

"Scoot."

Chapter Thirteen

"Well, Dan, you'll never in a million years guess what I did this afternoon. I'm still kinda shocked myself, but I admit I feel a rush of pride, too, holding my own with all those younger women. The class wasn't cheap, but it wasn't a bad price for Lauren's increased confidence. Money well spent, I think, for that result. And maybe she'll be more respectful.

You see, Bay spilled her juice last week. She's refusing to use a lidded cup anymore. I asked Larkin to get under the couch and wipe up the spill, and Lauren sneered at me. Actually sneered, with the corner of her mouth curled up like your sister Bethany always does.

She said, "You'd better do it, Larkin. Mom's not flexible enough to get under things herself. She's getting old, you know, and it won't be long before she'll be in a rocking chair like somebody's great grandma." Then she walked out of the room as calmly as if she'd said today is Wednesday, just stating a fact.

I admit I haven't found a new yoga studio since the move, but I'm not inflexible. I just had my arms full at the time. And you know my best comebacks always occur to me hours too late. Anyway, I didn't say a word, but when I saw that ad for a one-day Intro to Trapeze class at the community college over in Ableville, I signed us both up, me and the sarcastic one. Margaret offered to keep an eye on the other girls while we were at the class. I think she thought it was *funny, but she didn't raise a daughter like Lauren, either.*

Julie set the platter of French toast on the table. "Girls, eat up and tackle your Saturday chores quickly. Lauren, you and I have an appointment at eleven o'clock. Margaret is coming over to keep an eye on the rest of you. She said she'll teach you how to make little pies." She picked up her fork, not making eye contact with Lauren.

"Mother, I have homework. I can't go with you," Lauren complained. "What did you have planned, anyway?"

"I'm not telling you, but you'll want to wear clothes you can move around in. Those blue leggings would be good."

"Some dumb project, I bet." Lauren frowned. "I told Emily we could study together at noon."

"Tell Emily you'll be back around one." Julie cut up Bay's peach slice. "You'll be a good girl for Margaret, right?"

"Where are we going?" Lauren's voice was sharp. "Why are you constantly trying to run my life?"

"Yeah, Mom, where are you and Lauren going?" Savannah chimed in. "Why can't I come?"

"Not this time. You'll enjoy making pies more than what we're going to do anyway." Julie kept her face straight. "More fruit, anyone?"

Twenty minutes later, Julie placed the last plate in the dishwasher and rinsed her hands. *What have I got myself into?* She sighed. *I can't let the girls get the upper hand, not when I'm this outnumbered. If Dan were here, he'd say I have nothing to prove to anyone, but he's gone and Lauren needed to be put in her place. It'll be a good thing, so long as neither of us gets hurt.* She headed upstairs to put on her leotards on under her jeans.

In the van, Lauren badgered, insisting her mother tell her where they were headed, but Julie refused to so much as give a hint.

"I've sensed some disrespect from you lately, and I'm hoping this experience will help you see me in a new light. I have feelings, too, you know."

"Really, Mother." Lauren sighed. "Is this one of those scared-straight things? Are we going to the jailhouse or what?"

"Relax. It might be fun, you never know."

"Mother, just tell me!"

The ride to Abelville was quiet after that, each lost in her own thoughts.

I hope my years of gymnastics training come back to me. That was so long ago.

Mother doesn't remember what it was like to be young, to have a life of her own

I've birthed five children—what am I thinking? Maybe she's right, maybe I am getting old.

I wish Daddy was alive; he could run interference, make Mother understand me more.

If Dan was alive, I'd never do this. He'd sit Lauren down for a talking to, they'd come away laughing and that would be that.

I bet Mother is just doing this to scare me. Maybe I've been a bit rude lately. I bet we're going to the Mall of America shopping. Maybe an arts and crafts class. She knows I like painting.

I hope I don't break my neck. Who'll take care of the kids if I get hurt?

"Mother, you missed the turn off to the city." Lauren asked, "We're going shopping, right?"

"Not today. I told you we have an appointment. We're going to Ableville." Julie's hands tightened on the steering wheel, matching the tightness in her stomach.

"What is there to do in that podunk town? It's even smaller than Wilsonville."

Julie took the next exit and turned down a side street. "We're going to the community college. Did you know they have clown classes? Barnum and Bailey used to train aerialists here."

"Barnum and what?" Lauren puzzled. "We're going to see clowns?"

"Oh, no, not today." She put the van in park. "Hop out, we're here."

"We're where?" Lauren stared at the nondescript steel building. "There aren't any signs."

Julie picked up her gym bag, took a deep breath and headed for the door. What had she read about the Act As If principle? *Come on, Self, act as if you know what you're doing.* She pushed open the door and ushered Lauren inside.

Lauren took two steps in and froze in disbelief.

"Move, Lauren, I can't close the door." Julie urged, ignoring her own shaking knees. "I guess you weren't planning on a trapeze class this morning."

"I don't like this. You know I'm not big on heights. I don't want to watch people fling themselves around way high up." Lauren scanned the large open space. "Where are the bleachers?"

"No, we're not here to watch. I booked a session for us. You and me." She wiped her hands on her jeans and smiled as a young woman walked from the mat to them. "Hi, I'm Julie and this is my daughter, Lauren. We're ready."

"I'm not ready! Mother, we can't do this." Lauren clutched her bag tighter. "Are you crazy? You're always saying we can't do things that might get us hurt, and now…"

"Great, come with me. You can take off your outerwear here. I'm Casey, your instructor for the next couple of hours. The others are already here." Casey put her hands on her hips and surveyed Lauren. "Can you put down your bag or is it stuck to your body? Little uneasy, are we?"

"Excuse us a minute, my mother lost her mind." Lauren glared at the instructor. "She's always saying it's her job to keep us girls safe and now—"

"Sometimes we have to push back the walls a bit, Daughter, or they'll crush the light out of us." Julie stripped off her sweater. "Come on, this will be fun."

"Mother! Leotards? What if someone sees you in that outfit?"

"They'll think I'm here to learn. Kick off your boots; you can't walk a tightrope in boots."

"A *tightrope?*"

"You'll be fine. We have safety nets." Casey grinned, her ponytail flipping. "You're not going to let an old lady like your mother show you up, are you?"

Laurens stared at her mother, willing her to give up and take her shopping or out to lunch instead.

Julie bit her bottom lip, but met her daughter's eyes. "Honey, if you're too scared, you don't have to try. I paid for a class, but I can just tell your sisters you didn't want to do it. Casey, I'm ready when you are."

"No *way*. If you can do it, I can do it." Lauren flung her coat on the bench, peeled off her jeans and walked across the thick mat toward three twenty-somethings.

"Ladies, this is Julie and Lauren, newbies, come to show us what they got. Let's get started, shall we?"

"See, the thing is, if you can walk on it here, it's no different up there. You can use a pole to help keep your center of gravity…well, centered, over your feet." Casey demonstrated how to walk on a tightrope suspended eight inches off the floor. "And don't look down. You already know where your feet are. Keep your eyes on the goal, the platform at the end. Who's up first?" Casey laughed as Julie's hand shot up followed immediately by Lauren's.

Three hours later, Julie hugged Holly, Savannah and Larkin. "Thanks for watching them, Margaret. Is Bay napping?"

"Yes, your little one is plumb worn out, she played so hard." Margaret smiled, "Oh, my, we had us a good time, didn't we, girls? Show your mama your pies, then let us have a minute to talk, all right?"

"It was something, all right." Lauren brushed past the adults on her way to her bedroom. "I have homework to do."

After the girls showed off their pies, still cooling, they ran to play.

Margaret sat down by Julie in the airy kitchen. "How was your class? I want to hear all about it. My, I don't think I would have been brave enough for a tightrope walk back in my day."

"It was incredible!" Julie let out a deep breath. "Once in a lifetime, because once is plenty for me. But you would have been proud of me, Margaret. After a quick demonstration on the floor, they had us walk across a real tightrope and back, about thirty feet long, with a long pole in hand to help us balance.

Lauren went first, and I could see she was terrified, but trying not to show it. That bar in her hands shook so hard, I was afraid it'd knock her off balance, and it was a long drop to the safety net below."

She took a breath. "When my turn came, I commanded my knees to quit knocking and I…well, I can't say I skipped along or did any fancy moves, but I made it across without falling, and pretty fast, too. I kept thinking, I birthed five daughters, so how hard can walking across a tightrope be? After all, if that rope was stretched flat on a floor, I wouldn't have had any trouble getting across it. Mind tricks, you know?"

Margaret shook her head in disbelief. "I swan."

"At the end, I stepped on the little platform and Lauren clung to me in a bear hug. I think she was actually worried about me," Julie confided. "The instructor said we'd be trying a trapeze pass-off next, and she called on us to do it first! There I was, hanging by my middle-aged knees. Even upside down, I could see a light in Lauren's eyes. You know how determined she gets. We swung back and forth, back and forth, until we were close enough for me to grab her wrists. Good thing she's so slim; transferring her weight about pulled my arms out of socket. We swung twice, then dropped to the net and landed in a tangle. The other class members applauded, the instructor complimented us, and I haven't heard Lauren laugh that much in weeks. She was probably relieved I didn't land on her. I'm more sore than I'll ever admit and I have no desire to go back for part two, but I think she has a little more respect for me now. How dare she call me Old!"

"I'm proud of you, Julie. I don't think you could have done that when you first moved here." Margaret raised her voice. "Girls? The pies should be cool enough to eat. Who wants to try them?"

Chapter Fourteen

Lauren assured Julie she could watch the girls the following Saturday afternoon. "Go, Mother, the break will do you good, and none of us want to spend hours at a boring old library basement."

"You're sure? It's just that since we moved here, I've been fascinated by the legend of the Civil Ward gold possibly transiting through town." Julie fidgeted with her button. "Bay can be a handful. Maybe I'd better take her with me."

"Yeah, right, like you expect her to stay silent in a room full of dusty old newspapers. Go." Lauren handed her mother her blue coat. "And take your time."

Within half an hour, Julie squinted over an old ledger, cotton archivist's gloves on her hands. She settled in to make out the old script on page eighteen with a contented sigh.

Back home, Lauren ruled her realm like any good dictator. "Bribes, rewards, whatever you want to call it, nobody's having any fun until this place is tidy. Mother's not going to come home to a mess on my watch, get it? You, Larkin, get the breakfast dishes done and mop the kitchen floor. Holly, clean up in front of the fireplace and sweep the hearth. That wood makes such a mess. Savannah, both upstairs bathrooms are your responsibility. Bay, come help me put away these blocks." Lauren knelt by the toybox and glanced up. No one had moved.

"Get a move on!" she barked. "You can all go out and play in the yard once this place is cleaned up. And not until. Hurry up. How many more perfect autumn days will we get?"

Holly and Larkin scattered. Bay slowly picked up a wooden block and dropped it in the bin.

"You can't tell me what to do, you know." Savannah stood her ground, arms crossed furrowed. "I'm not one of the little kids."

Lauren laughed dryly. "Sure, I can, unless you want me to casually mention to Mother what you said to Emily Jane at school—"

"You wouldn't! You're a tyrant *and* a snitch." Savannah stalked off.

"Come on, Bay, when all the blocks are in the box, we'll line up all the toy cars." Lauren smiled, sure the place would be tidied in no time. Or "redd up," as they say in Michigan. She was debating about serving lunch on the sunny front porch, although the temperature wasn't picnic weather, when Savannah came back into the room and sat on the loveseat beside the toybox.

"Get back to work," Lauren ordered, "or you won't get any free time at all today." When Savannah didn't move, she glanced up. "Are you sick? Your face is a funny color."

Savannah said slowly, "One of the kids got hurt and didn't say anything. It's…bad."

"Who's hurt?" Lauren sat back on her heels. "What are you talking about?"

"I went to empty the waste bin in the upstairs bathroom and there was a washcloth covered in blood tucked under a plastic bag."

"Nobody's hurt, Savannah. You're so dramatic." Laurent sniffed. "If one of the girls were hurt, they'd have raised a ruckus, you know how they are. Were there any bandage wrappers in the trash?"

"No."

"See? It's probably red marker or paint or something. The kids are always into some mess or another." Lauren pointed. "Back to work and do a good job on the tubs."

"Don't you have a soul?" Savannah snapped. "How can you let one of our own sisters hide an injury and not even care?"

"Oh, all right, but don't think this will get you out of your chores." Lauren called, "Girls, come in here." She lined them up on the couch and stared them down. "Who knows about red stuff in the bathroom?" Holly and Bay stared back, but Larkin dropped her eyes, her cheeks flaming. "Ah, ha. Okay, you two, take a break, find a toy or something, and don't leave the kitchen until I say you can. Larkin, stay right there."

Tears slid down Larkin's face. "I didn't know...there was some blood, but it doesn't hurt and I..."

"Nothing to be embarrassed about, Larkin. Come upstairs, we'll get you some supplies and then we'll have a talk, okay?" Lauren put her arm around her sister. "You're okay, you're not dying and you're not in trouble. This is perfectly normal and natural. You don't have to hide it from us or anything. We're girls, too." They headed upstairs, detoured to the bathroom, then perched on Larkin's bed.

"You remember that book Mom showed you last summer? Lauren, get the book. That's what's happening. You're one of the big girls now." Savannah said. "Most girls call it a period; we call it a punctuation point."

"I heard you tell Mom to pick up some punctuation point stuff when she went to the store last week." Larkin ventured a smile. "I was so confused."

"Yeah, that's it. It's nothing to be embarrassed about, but it's kinda personal, you know?"

Lauren thumbed to page 318 in the anatomy book. "See, your body has a cycle, about twenty-eight days long. Everything living has cycles; trees, seasons, plants in the garden, the earth itself. It's just replacing cells, laying down fresh ones. Did you know your stomach lining replaces itself every few days? It's a cool process."

"It's your body gearing up to be a mother someday. When I started, Mom told me my granddaughters and great-great-granddaughters were watching me, happy that I have a healthy body." Savannah hugged Larkin. "You might feel crummy for a day or so. You can talk to Mom and she'll give you a heating pad and let you skip chores. Don't do that too often, though, or she'll see right through you."

"What about Holly?"

"You two are sisters, not carbon copies. Her turn will come, and when it does, you can reassure her." Lauren wagged a finger. "Just don't lord it over her; you're so competitive. Now get back to work."

"I might not be feeling so good," Larkin simpered.

"That's quite a dramatic act." Lauren punched her on the arm. "Fine, you go sit by Bay and encourage her to pick up her toys and I'll finish the kitchen with Savannah."

Chapter Fifteen

Four months later

"Okay, kids, enough moping around the house like a bunch of dust mops. You're wasting a perfectly good January afternoon. The sun is shining, and it's a pretty day for playing outdoors." Julie swatted Larkin's shoulder as she passed with an armload of folded towels.

"M-o-o-o-o-m-m," Larkin grumbled, turning another page in her Nancy Drew book.

"Mother, have you noticed the thermometer? It was one degree below zero, last I looked." Lauren tossed her notebook aside. "Humans can't breathe air that cold, you know."

Julie surveyed her daughters with a frown. "I think they can, and we'll find out as soon as I get Bay up from her nap. What you all need is some fresh air to get your blood circulating. I have an idea. We're going skating." At a wail from the toddler's room, Julie bounded up the stairs, ignoring the protests from her daughters below.

Above the complaints, Holly's voice rose. "Yippee! Mom found a roller-skating place. I hope it's warm inside."

"Silly goose, she thinks we're going to ice skate outdoors, on the lake. I heard one of the women in the store telling her they make a big deal of it on Saturdays. We'll freeze to death before dinner. Mother is getting pretty bossy these days." Lauren snorted. "I, for one, am not going."

"Yes, you are, we're all going." Julie came downstairs with a bright-eyed Bay in her arms. "I found a crate of skates in the lean-to last week and Josiah sharpened them. I thought you'd enjoy learning to ice skate, and today's the day. Come on, you guys, get ready. It'll be fun."

"I want to come with you, Mommy," Holly snuggled close to Julie. "I like fun."

"Good, now go get your snow pants on, and your red jacket." Julie smiled at Larkin. "Bundle up, then help round up mittens, please. Savannah, will you bring me Bay's snowsuit while I change her diaper?"

As the girls scrambled to get ready, Lauren turned back to her magazine. "I'm not coming. You can't make me."

"I can't *make* you? What are you, five?" Julie buttoned Bay's romper and locked eyes with her eldest. "This is a family excursion, and I'd like you to join us."

"No." Lauren tossed her head.

"Suit yourself." Julie pulled a green sweater over Bay's head, eliciting a giggle. "Where's my little girl? *There* you are!"

"We look like a marshmallow family." Ten minutes later, Julie tucked Larkin's wool scarf over her lower face. "That'll protect your cheeks from the wind. Everybody ready? Hop in the van."

"I need to go to the bathroom."

"Really, Holly? Why didn't you go before you put everything on? Hurry up." Julie sighed. "The rest of you, unzip your jackets so you don't overheat while we wait."

A few minutes later as Julie buckled Bay's car seat strap, Lauren ran out, zipping her blue coat.

"I thought you were going to stay here." Julie glanced at her daughter's face. "Are you okay? You're white as a sheet."

"My sheets have flowers on them," Holly chirped.

"Stripes are better than flowers," Larkin decreed.

"Are not!"

"Yes, they *are*. Stripes are the best."

"No, they're not!"

"Knock it off back there, you two." Julie asked Lauren, "Are you alright?"

"I...I...That is...I just decided to come with you all." Lauren climbed in the front passenger seat, her face set. "Is that all right?"

"Of course, I'm glad you're here. It's just that your voice sounded a little off." Julie called, "Everybody in? Let's go!"

Snow flurries swirled as Julie maneuvered the van down the driveway. She glanced at Lauren's face. "Okay, Lauren, the lake's not far, so if you have something on your mind, spill it."

"It's nothing, really." Lauren stared out the side window. "I just…I thought I heard—Oh, it's nothing."

"Okay, but if you want to tell me something, I'm here." Julie glanced in the rearview mirror and raised her voice. "Girls, when we park, we'll go to the warming shed to put our skates on, that big tent on the shore. You older girls, I'll need your help with all the laces, okay? Oh, look at all the people skating. I told you this is a perfect day for it."

A few minutes later, all the girls, except Bay, had skates on and they were itching to get on the ice.

"Mom, there's a girl from the church, see her over there? Can I go over by her?" At a nod, Larkin took off across the ice, feet splaying, but upright.

"I want to try skating, Mom, but I'll be back soon to help watch Bay, okay?" Savannah careened across the ice, her arms flapping like a wayward windmill.

"Lauren, will you hold Holly's hand until she gets her feet under her? I don't want to take Bay out in the cold more than I have to."

Lauren nodded. As she moved toward the door of the warming house, she turned back. "Mother, I…Back at the house, I thought I heard Dad's voice telling me to get off the couch and come with you, that you needed me. It sounded just like him." Grasping Holly's hand, Lauren darted onto the ice, her cheeks flushed.

Lauren walked with Bay to the doorway. "See, honey, the girls are going round and round. In couple of years, you'll be out there with them. Meanwhile, I need to keep an eye on that biggest sister of yours. Lauren's not one for hearing voices." She pulled Bay's stocking cap over her ears. "But if your daddy was here, he'd be the first one on the ice."

"Julie McCain? I thought those were your girls out there. The one in the purple coat is a natural. That age, they don't have any fear. Fine day for skating, isn't it?" Two women greeted Julie. "You'll stay for chili later on, won't you? Old Marcus has a vat of it on the fire, big enough for half the town."

Julie smiled, trying to recall their names. "I wondered what smelled so good."

"When you're ready to try the ice, I'd be pleased to mind your little one for you. I'm Meg, by the way, and Joann here. There were so many people at your place on the day you moved in, I expect the names ran together like grease on a skillet."

"Thanks, I'm afraid I missed most of them. I do recall some of the old timers from when I used to visit my aunt Tansy." Julie smiled. "Being here brings back memories. I skated here when I was a child, and now my own kids are on the ice."

"There you go, and the rest of us will be friends in no time. Why don't you get out there with them? See if you still got the moves, as the young people say."

"Up." Bay reached up her arms to Meg. "Up."

Meg beamed. "Oh, you sweet child. Want to see what I have my pockets while Mommy sees how fast skating will come back to her?" She nodded to Julie. "You run along now. We'll be fine here."

"Are you sure?" Julie raised a brow. "I'll glance in every round. If she gives you any trouble, you flag me down." With a grateful nod, Julie tightened her skates and took to the ice. She sailed past Lauren and Holly, pleased to see them picking up speed. As she circled, she spotted Larkin, holding hands in a wobbly chain with three other girls. A few feet away, Savannah waved and took a spill, her face sheepish. Julie waved back.

Ah, freedom! The icy wind bit at her face, her body snug in her parka. The only thing missing was Dan at her side. They'd skated quite a bit in their early years, arms linked, his breath warm in her ear. She could almost feel his hand in hers, muffled by thick gloves. She shook off the memory as tears came to her eyes. The last thing she needed was her eyelashes frozen together. The temperature was dropping and, this time of year, dusk came early.

Reaching Lauren and Holly, Julie slowed and circled them.

"Mom, will you show me how you do that? I want to skate backwards, too." Lauren nodded toward a group of teens. "Later, I mean. Is it okay if I go meet those kids over there?"

"Sure, have a good time." Julie's eyes swept the ice, counting noses. All accounted for. "There you go, Holly, you're doing great. Let's see how far you can go without holding my hand, okay? Keep your blades straight, a little faster, and—Whoa!" Four older teens raced by, elbows tight, their skates skimming the ice. "Not that fast, okay?"

Forty minutes later, spotlights flashed on and off and on again. Marcus clanged a wooden spoon against a pot lid in front of the large warming shed. "Come and get it!" As one, the skaters headed toward the warming shed, spilling like beads on a necklace into the warming shed.

Laughing, red faced, Julie's daughters gathered around her.

"Mommy, those people are eating with their ice skates on! Do I have to take mine off?" Holly asked.

"No, Honey, when in Rome, as they say. Get some food and find a place at the tables. Just tell me before you head back out onto the ice, all of you, please. It'll be dark soon."

Holly giggled. "Supper with ice skates on is funny."

"So is eating in a big tent with snow under the table." Larkin and Savannah linked arms and headed toward the line forming for chili and cornbread. Soon the family joined others at a long table.

Savannah warmed her hands over her steaming bowl of chili. "Mmmmm…my favorite." She smiled. "Mom, this was a great idea."

"May we join you?" A family Julie had noticed on the ice settled alongside them. A lively conversation broke out. The weather, how were they settling in, what about the sale at the market. "Batteries; we always need more batteries in case the power goes out."

Julie broke off another piece of cornbread for Bay. Where was Lauren? She glanced out the open doorway and saw a group of teens gathering, forming a line, Lauren's green wool cap among them. *Good, she needs to make friends.* "Yes, Larkin, you may get more chili. Sure, Holly, if you ate your chili all gone, you can get a brownie. Mr Marcus is a good cook, isn't he?"

"Oh, I don't like this, not one bit," a woman down the table exclaimed. Other heated voices chimed in. "They're doing it again."

"What's going on?" Julie asked.

"Those big kids, they've been warned over and over not to play crack-the-whip. Somebody's going to get hurt one of these days. They hold on and get going too fast to let loose. It's dangerous."

Just as Julie stood to call to Lauren to come back, Larkin tipped over her cup of cider. Julie mopped it with a stack of paper napkins and blotted her coat. "Don't worry, it's washable and I—" Julie turned as the group gasped.

Voices mingled. "That little girl!"

"Whose is she?"

"Somebody grab her!"

"Don't they see her? They're going too fast to stop!"

Julie's eyes skimmed her daughters, counting automatically. Bay was beside her, Lauren was out on the ice, Larkin right here, Savannah by the chili pot—

Where is Holly? She spun, but didn't see her.

The skates flashed faster and faster, the teens at the end of the line shouting, unable to stop, afraid to let go. Someone screamed as the chain swung wildly toward a small red-coated child alone in the shadows at the far end of the ice.

A red coat...

Holly's red coat.

No...Not my daughter!

The skaters went down in a tangle of skates and scarves, shouts and cries. Adults skimmed the ice, racing to help the skaters. As if to mask the scene, snowflakes fell faster, swirling in the streetlight's glare.

Julie shouted, "Savannah, your sisters—" before skating onto the smooth ice, a cold sweat gripping her center.

"I got them, Mom!" Savannah called. "Go!"

By the time Julie reached the teens, most of them were on their feet, panting, faces ashen. A knot of people surrounded a child, prone on the rink, blood dripping from a gash on her head, freezing as it hit the ice, the crimson liquid matching her red parka.

A keening shriek came from Lauren as she knelt, pulling at the little red coat. Her face stricken, she wailed, "Mom, I'm so sorry! I couldn't stop, I tried not to hit her, Mom, I've killed Holly!"

Chapter Sixteen

Minutes oozed by as slowly as cold caramel. Julie cradled Holly's limp body, rocking her baby, applying pressure with her gloved hand on the red gash in her matted hair. "Holly, honey, open your eyes. Wake up, my sweet girl." Four minutes later or a week later, she couldn't tell, the quiet of the dusk was broken by the wail of an ambulance.

Their voices low, two EMTs pried Holly from Julie's arms and strapped her onto a too-white gurney. Julie climbed in the ambulance, her eyes skimming the silent crowd. "Lauren, watch your sis—"

Lauren doubled over, sobbing, while Savannah awkwardly patting her back.

"It's okay, Mom." Savannah's solemn eyes met Julie's. "I've got them."

Meg passed Julie's shoes into the ambulance. "You'll want these. Not to worry, Julie. We'll take care of your girls. We'll see to it they get home. You tend to the one who needs you."

Lauren's blotchy face, blurred with tears, was the last thing Julie saw as the ambulance pulled away, its siren filling the space of eternity. She clung to Holly's hand as the EMTs undid her coat, pulled off her mittens, rigged up wires and monitors, shone a light in her eyes.

"You're Mrs McCain, yes?" A uniformed woman reached across Holly to shake her hand. "I'm Emmy. I run the inn south of town and work in the med center part time. Dr Simms is already on his way; he'll meet us there. Can you tell me what happened?"

"The ice…crack-the-whip…There's so much blood. Why won't she wake up?" Julie swiped at a tear rolling down her face. "Holly, Mommy's here. Wake up, okay?"

"Holly, is it? Looks like she bumped her head. Heads bleed a lot. It's probably not as bad as it looks. Should have put ice on it right away, but I guess she did that, huh?" Emmy's lame attempt at humor fell flat. "Listen, you're in luck. Dr Simms is from the city. He helps out here for two months every winter, says he likes to keep his hand in and be close to the ice fishing. I bet Holly here will be just fine, probably needs a few stitches is all. Dr Simms is a neurosurgeon who knows all there is to know about head injuries. We're lucky to have him." She raised her voice. "Hey, Jimmy, pick up the pace, will you? You drive like your grandpa."

Julie knew the tiny medical center closed at four o'clock. Not today: Light spilled onto the snow from double doors gaped wide. Three people in scrubs barreled across the icy sidewalk before the ambulance fully stopped.

"Now, who have we here? Cute little snippet, isn't she?" The man extended his hand to Julie, his eyes locked on Holly. "Joseph Simms. Good to meet you. Sorry about the reason. Let's get your little girl fixed up, shall we? Nasty cut on her head." He reached for the proffered clipboard. "Vitals not too bad."

One of the nurses led Julie to a chair as the others unloaded the gurney and wheeled Holly into the medical center. She knelt before Julie. "I'm sorry, I need to ask you some questions, but can we get your skates off first?" She untied Julie's laces. "Please sit still a moment. I need you to take these skates off."

Julie numbly set her shoes down. "I need to be with Holly —"

"I know. You can go in there in just a minute. Dr Simms knows what he's doing. Other foot. There you go. I'm Candy, by the way." She stood. "Now, tell me, how old is Holly? Date of birth? You folks live at the old Glyth House, right? I know your address. Insurance? Is there someone who can come be with you? Where is her father?"

Julie shook her off. "I can't—I need to be with—"

"Just a few more questions."

The outer door flew open, the glass resounding as it hit the wall. "Julie, dear, we came as soon as we heard. I didn't want you to be alone. We're here, dear." Margaret wrapped her arms around Julie.

"Margaret, Josiah! My girls…"

"Not to worry your head, now. They're home safe and sound and the church ladies are spoiling them as we speak." Josiah patted Julie's shoulder. "Now, how's our little Holly?"

"I don't know. They—"

Dr Simms came through the swinging doors, his face giving nothing away. "Mrs McCain, please sit down, all of you. Margaret, Josiah, good of you to be here." He patted Julie's hand. "Your Holly has a good laceration on her head. Looks like she might have hit a skate blade. I've told those kids and told them…" He cleared his throat. "I stitched it closed. Once her hair covers it, you won't even see a scar. I'm not too concerned about the cut. But our girl isn't awake yet. Probably some concussion. I'd like to keep her overnight. Want to keep an eye on her."

"I'm not leaving her."

"Of course not. Best thing when she wakes up will be to see her mother. We'll set up a roll-away for you. And I'll be here all night, down the hall. You can call me if you need anything or want to chat."

"Thank you, Doctor."

"Call me Joseph. Do you want to see Holly now?" Dr Simms took Julie's hand.

Chapter Seventeen

Julie stood over Holly's bed, taking in the too-familiar hospital smell. Holly's face was just a few shades darker than the stark white sheets. A thick gauze dressing rested against her tangled curls. Julie drew a deep breath, forcing images of previous hospital rooms from her mind. *This is Holly, not Dan. Holly will be alright, she'll be home soon. Not like Dan...*

"Holly, baby, Mommy's here. You're going to be okay." She cleared her throat and took Holly's soft hand in hers. "Can you open your eyes?"

A monitor beeped and spit out a length of paper ribbon, pooling on the floor. Tears filled Julie's eyes. "Doctor, is it okay that she isn't awake?"

"Joseph, call me Joseph, like I said. Let's step out, shall we? We medical types aren't sure what unconscious patients can hear."

In the hallway, Joseph continued. "Didn't want to Holly to overhear. A colleague of mine had a patient threaten to sue him. Simple knee surgery, and the doctor got hiccups. He said, 'Uh, oh, this is not good.' On some level, the man heard that. Panicked, figuring the surgery was going badly. He came out of anesthesia is a tizzy, let me tell you."

"Is Holly okay?" Julie pressed.

"Well, I'd expect her to be alert by now. That's why I want to keep her here overnight. I checked her top to toe. Good reflexes, and her pupils are even. Only thing I can find is that cut on her head. It's pretty deep, but it closed nicely. She might be doing what her body needs, extra sleep so she can heal. The body is a remarkable thing. I'd say by breakfast, she'll be good as new. With a headache, no doubt, but kids bounce back fast."

"Doctor Simms, Mayo Clinic's trauma center is returning your call." A nurse poked her head out of a doorway.

"The Mayo Clinic?" Julie gasped. "You said you're not worried!"

"Now, now, Julie, I'm working on a paper on head trauma. My turn for playing phone tag." He smiled reassuringly. "I'm being honest."

"Come on, Mrs McCain, you can sit with your daughter." The nurse, Candy, cocked her head at Josiah. "Maybe you could help me warm up that hot cocoa in the lounge. I have some cookies, too."

Josiah shook his head, "You don't need me…"

The nurse pulled at his arm, and he nodded, realizing she was allowing Margaret space to talk to Julie.

Margaret patted Julie's hand as they settled into two straight back chairs beside Holly's bed. "You poor dear, this is very difficult for you. But Holly is a strong, happy child. In a couple of days, this will all be behind you. Soon she'll forget this ever happened."

"I keep thinking about her father. That antiseptic smell. After his accident, he was in a room a lot like this one and I keep thinking…"

"I remember Tansy telling me about you. That was the month she'd had her foot surgery and she was so upset at missing the funeral. She loved you so much. I know she lost sleep those days after your man's accident." Margaret straightened her back. "And I'm sure you're worried about little Holly. You need to remind yourself that she's not like your husband. She's a sturdy little girl with a knot on her head. She'll be just fine."

"I wish Dan was here. My heart hurts, missing him. I guess I leaned on him more than I knew. My parents died just a few years after we married, and he was such a strength to me."

"You've been through a lot. I know Tansy was shook up when she heard of the plane crash. You weren't old enough to lose both parents."

"Not much older than Lauren, really. Dan was such a support." Julie swiped at a tear. "I guess I never quite got my feet under me, and now I have no one to lean on. No one at all."

"Now, now, you have us, and we love you." Margaret stood as Candy rolled in a folding cot. Josiah followed with a tray of hot cocoa and cookies.

"It's getting late. Some nice warm cocoa will help you relax enough to sleep." Margaret passed Julie a cup. "Once you're settled, Josiah will go check on your daughters. I'll be right outside in the hallway."

A few minutes later, Julie stood on tiptoe and kissed the old man's cheek. "Give that to my girls, will you? Tell them we'll be home soon."

Josiah touched his cheek. "If I can make my way through the mob of church ladies, I'll do that. You get some rest now. You'll see, Holly will be fine in the morning."

But she wasn't.

Chapter Eighteen

In her troubled sleep, Julie dreamed she was standing beside Dan's hospital bedside. A cardboard-cut out of her mother insisted, "Hurry it up. They have to take his body away. He can't hear you anyway, he's dead. Pull yourself together, Julie. This is no time for being dramatic."

Julie clung to Dan's hand. "Don't leave me! I need you! How can I raise the girls alone?"

Dan closed one eye in a lazy wink. "I gotta go, Beloved. You can do this. You can teach them all they need to know, one daughter at a time." His eyes closed, he reached out his hand and rested it on Julie's arm. "And this one, she's a fighter."

The beeping of monitors grew louder until Julie realized she was no longer dreaming. A figure bent over the hospital bed in the wan dawn light.

She sat up, her back stiff from the lumpy cot. "Holly? Is she—"

"Sorry to wake you, Mrs McCain. I was trying to be quiet," Dr Simms whispered. "No change yet, I'm afraid. Still unresponsive."

Julie stood beside the bed. "What about—?"

"Come with me." They walked out into the dimly lit hall.

"I can't say why she's still not responding. From what I can tell, there's nothing wrong beyond a bump on her head. There might be more damage, but without more sophisticated equipment, I can't be sure." He swept his arm, taking in the small-town clinic.

"Should she be in a bigger hospital?"

"I thought about that, but I can't see transporting her until I know more. Besides, if they called in a specialist, that would be me." He smiled. "I'm still thinking it's just a mild concussion. If I'm right, we'll know more today. Stay nearby if you can. You can bet she'll be confused when she wakes up."

"But she's going to be okay, right?"

"How are you at praying?"

The nurse brought breakfast on a tray and lunch later on, but Julie didn't touch either meal. Margaret stayed just out of sight, and Julie was dimly aware of the older woman quietly greeting curious visitors and sending them away. A few times, she brought in vases of flowers, setting them on the counter across from Holly's bed.

Julie stood at the window watching white snow fall, unconcerned, slowly smothering the world in a white coverlet. The wan light matched the bleak chill in her chest. As they often did, her thoughts turned to Dan.

Listen, I can't handle this alone. We made a promise on our wedding day to be together. If you can't be here with me, can you at least pull some strings up there for our little girl? Ask somebody for help, will you? She smiled, remembering how confidently Dan always refused to ask for directions, yet knowing he could talk to anybody, anywhere. She envied that trait and confided once that she didn't like being around strangers.

Dan had told her to try to make a connection as soon as she met anyone. "That way, they're not strangers anymore, see?"

Where are you now, when I need you, when Holly needs you? Look, Dan, you're in heaven, closer to God, right? Please, see if you can't snag a passing angel or someone to help our daughter, will you? We just need a small miracle here.

Later in the afternoon, Margaret came in, guided Julie to a chair and handed her a warm damp washcloth. "Now, dear, you need to rest. You haven't left her side all day."

Julie gratefully swiped the warm cloth on her face. "Thanks, this is just what I needed. Oh, Margaret, what if Holly doesn't wake up? What if her brain is damaged? She's so smart—"

"Don't think like that. What did Joseph say when he was in here a while ago?"

"He said she's stable. He thinks she should be awake, but she isn't. I've talked to her, sung songs she likes, I even shook her. I've done all I know how to do, but Holly's eyes just don't open. Oh, Margaret, what if—"

"What iffing never got nobody anywhere. We have to trust the doctor. All those years of medical school, he knows a lot." Margaret asked, "Are your in-laws coming to be with you? I know you said you were going to call them, let them know what's happened."

Julie shook her head. "I tried to call Dan's parents, but his sister said he's not able to travel after his bypass surgery and his wife won't leave his side. I told Dan's sister about the accident and she lit into me. Said raising the girls is too much for me, and what was I thinking, letting a child go out on a frozen lake in the first place? Said I had my head in the clouds, not a fit mother." She turned away, blotting a tear.

"Pshaw! Nonsense. Those girls are lucky to have you. Blessed, they are. Now, now, she was just wrong-headed in that." Margaret patted her hand. "What did you say to her?"

"I said—"

"I hope you told her to smarten up and let us handle the situation." Dr Simms shrugged on a white lab coat as he entered the room. "Your sister-in-law called here, too. Guess she figured I'd tell her more than you had. Every heard of patient confidentiality? On her third call to the med center in less than ten minutes, I told her to leave you alone, that she'd best count herself lucky if you don't block her number. You're a fine mother. I've seen the way you care for

Holly." He checked a softly beeping monitor and ran his hand over Holly's forehead. "She'll be awake soon, I feel sure of it. Meanwhile, I'd better go return some calls." With a nod, he closed the door behind him.

"I'm glad you're here." Julie took the older woman's soft hand. "It's just that I…" She jumped up at the sound of raised voices in the hallway. "Oh, no, that's Lauren."

"I'll see to her," Margaret said, but Julie was already opening the door.

"Lauren, what on earth? Keep your voice down."

"Oh, Mother, it's all my fault!" Lauren barreled into Julie's arms. "I should have stopped those kids. Dad never let me play crack-the-whip, but I wanted to be one of them, you know? I never saw Holly until it was too late. And now my sister…Mother, is she okay? Josiah said she's still not awake."

"Calm down, honey." Julie cupped her daughter's chin. "Have you even slept? Isn't that the sweater you had on yesterday?"

"It's all my fault. First Dad and now Holly and our family—" Lauren choked back a sob. "Is she going to die, too?"

Julie brushed the hair back from Lauren's face. "She's not going anywhere, not if I have a say in the matter. The doctor is concerned that Holly is still unresponsive but—"

"Now, now, you're going to scare young Holly." Margaret led them toward the door. "Let's move to the hall, shall we?"

Mother and daughter clung to each other in the hallway.

At last Julie spoke. "You know, everything we do on earth is in God's hands. Remember Dad used to sing that song, whatever will be, will be? We need to trust and have a little faith."

"I can't. If God loved us, he wouldn't take our Holly." Lauren lowered her eyes. "A woman who brought a casserole to the house said God must need her more than we do."

"God doesn't work like that, you know that. He loves his children, all of us and wants what's best for us." "We talked about this when your dad passed away, remember? God has a plan for each of us, and we get to make choices along the way, choices that lead us to Him or away from Him." Julie pulled Lauren to a couple of chairs. "Our main reasons for being away from heaven are to take on mortal experiences, build relationships, and learn all we need to to return to our Father. When He calls us home, however long we have on earth, well, that means we've done all we needed to do while we were away from our heavenly home. Dad accomplished that pretty early. Sometime when a child dies, I wonder if that means they just needed to experience a small taste of mortality, and that's enough."

"But Holly is so little—and it's my fault she got hurt and…"

"I know, honey, but let's think about this. Who lives life more enthusiastically than a six-year-old? You know Holly is close to God; she listens and wants to learn all she can and she tries so hard to be good and to help people. I'd say Holly is pretty close to perfection already."

"But Mother, I love her too much. I never tell her, but I do. She'd leave a hole in my heart forever if she…if she…"

Chapter Nineteen

"All right, you two, that's enough of that." Margaret moved closer with a small smile. "Joseph Simms says he's not worried, that he can't see anything wrong with young Holly. Nobody said she's packing her bags for the Pearly Gates." She nodded at Julie. "How about you head on home and check on your other girls? They're probably worried sick. Have supper together, then come on back. I'll stay here with Lauren. It'll do her good to sit with her sister. Josiah?"

"I'll run you over to the house, sure I will," Josiah came around the corner.

"I can't leave her—" Julie pulled her cardigan tighter.

"Yes, you can." Lauren squared her shoulders. "Go, Mother. I can watch over Holly. She's *my* sister. And see what you can do about Bay. At this rate, she'll be too spoiled to endure."

"What?" Julie raised an eyebrow.

"I don't think she's touched the floor since those ladies from the church arrived. They keep carrying her around and cooing over her. Somebody let her have apple pie for breakfast." Lauren snapped, "It's just *sickening.*"

Julie hugged her, chuckling for the first time in two days.

After Julie left, Lauren shooed Margaret out and paced around the hospital room. She plucked a tissue from the box, wiped her eyes, then held it up to the light. "Wood fibers? They could at least provide something soft around here." Hands on hips, she surveyed Holly, her body reaching only three-quarters of the way down the bed. She climbed up onto the too-white island and wrapped her arm around her sister. Holly's tangled hair tickled her face.

"God, if you're there like they say, I want you to listen to me," she whispered. "Can't you see what this is doing to Mom? She's a strong woman, everybody knows that, but how much more can she take? The preacher says You won't give us more than we can handle. You're getting awfully close to that line." She clutched Holly closer. "God, hear me out. You took our Dad, not caring that we needed him. I won't let you take my sister, I won't! She's just a little kid. You let Holly alone, do You hear me? You can't have her."

Lauren stroked Holly's peaceful face, unsure if her prayer would be answered. What had she done? Nobody threatens God. Maybe she'd be struck dead, like those people in the Bible who talked back to Him.

She stood and walked to the window, the inky evening sky devoid of stars. A few lazy snowflakes skittered in the streetlight's glow. Suddenly, a flash of brilliant light streaked across the heavens. She recoiled, blinking. *Oh, no, not me, too*, she thought. *Well, if You're going to take us, we're going together.* She leaped onto the bed and grabbed Holly, squeezing her eyes shut.

"Ouch! You're squishing me." Holly pushed Lauren's arm off her chest.

"Holly? Is that you?" Lauren sat upright. "Holly, you're awake!" She whooped, holding her tighter.

"And you're hurting my ears!" Holly protested.

Dr Simms raced in, Margaret on his heels.

The doctor grinned at Holly, hands on his hips. "Hi, there, young lady, good to meet you at last."

Margaret gasped, "Praise be!" and fumbled in her purse for her cell phone. "Wait until your mama gets her hands on you. Josiah," she said into the phone, "Josiah, God is good and little Holly is awake. Bring Julie here right away." She paused. "What's that you say? In the parking lot? Hurry on in, then."

"You're still squishing me," Holly whined. "Let go of me!"

"She's awake?" Candy hurried in, drying her hands on a towel. "Doctor, what do you need me to do?"

He waved her away. "I'll give her a once-over soon as I can pry her loose from her sister. Lauren, she's right; you *are* squishing her. Can you let me get a look at her, please?"

Lauren slid off the bed but kept one hand on Holly's arm. "Holly, are you really okay?"

"Why are you being so weird? I woked up. So what?" Holly squirmed under Dr Simms' stethoscope. "That's cold. Who are you? Where am I?

What was that bright light that hurt my eyes? It woked me up."

"We all saw that fireball, a meteorite, I'm guessing." He checked her pulse. "I'm a doctor. My name is Joseph. You had a fall on the ice, and you came here to rest a bit. What do you remember?"

"My head hurts. Ummm…We went skating and I ate chili in a big tent and Mommy said I could have a brownie. And I saw a big light and I woked up." She raised her hand to her head, perplexed. "Lauren, my headband is stuck. Take it off."

Lauren turned to the doctor. "Can I—?"

"Let me remove it, okay? Hold still, Holly, for just a minute." He unwound the white gauze dressing, admired the sutures on Holly's scalp, and smiled. "My mother taught me that blanket stitch. Looks great, if I do say so myself."

The door flew open as Julie darted in. "Holly, I'm so glad you're alright! How do you feel?"

"I have to go to the bathroom. And I'm hungry. Can I have more chili?"

Julie hugged her, tears streaming.

"Everybody keeps squishing me! Mommy, you're getting me all wet."

"What do you feel like eating? Yogurt, pudding, gelatin?" Candy offered.

"That's *baby* food," Holly snorted indignantly.

Candy asked, "Doctor, what do you think?"

"If Holly says she's hungry, give her whatever she wants." Dr Simms smiled broadly. "And find her a big brownie."

Chapter Twenty

"No, I'm telling you, Connor, she's right as rain." Several weeks later, Julie curled her feet under her in the big chair in Tansy's conservatory and spoke to the video screen on her lap top. "Holly said her head ached, but within a few days, you'd never know she was hurt at all. A miracle, that's what it was. She woke up right after that fireball streaked across the sky. A meteorite, the news reported."

She blew at a dust mote in the wan sunlight. "Holly is fine. Now, Bay is another issue. The people here in town were so good to us, bringing food and caring for the girls, and Bay got pretty spoiled. She threw some epic tantrums, even regressed to that whining voice, the one that goes right through me. I finally told her I can't understand whining, that my ears don't work that way. If she wanted me to listen, she'd have to use a big-girl voice. She sighs a lot, but I think she'll get back to normal before long."

"You're right, I am outnumbered." Julie sipped her juice. "Connor, are you really over your bypass surgery? That was a rough time, with you and Holly both in the hospital. I felt torn, like I needed to be in both places, but there's only one of me." She paused. "Yes, of course, you're welcome to come see us as soon as you can travel. Let me tell you about Larkin and Savannah. I tell you, some days I can feel grey hairs sprouting. Thick as thieves, those two; if Larkin doesn't come up with some way to get in trouble, Savannah will. I swear they feed off each other, like a miniature mischief-making think tank. I found a jar with a live field mouse in it under Larkin's bed last week. I don't know what she was thinking, but at least she cut holes in the lid."

She chuckled, listening. "No, I don't know where she found a field mouse this time of year, but she said it had to live inside so it wouldn't be cold. Are you sure you're really okay, Connor? A heart bypass is nothing to sneeze at, you know. Yes, I agree, sneezing would probably hurt more than the surgery did. Listen, I need some advice about the garden slope. There's water from that old spring pushing on it and I don't know how much freezing and thawing it can take before the whole thing slides down. A retaining wall? I don't know anything about those, but I can ask around and hire someone. Take care of yourself, okay? Don't forget I love you. Marsha, too."

Margaret called through the kitchen door. "Julie? Can I come in? I brought you some fresh muffins."

"Thanks, come on in. They look wonderful." Julie sat in a kitchen chair, her face pale, a bath towel on her lap.

"Are you well, dear? You look a mite peaked."

"I just had something weird happen and I'm still thinking about it." Julie traced her finger across the table. "Actually, I'm doing all I can to not think about it."

"What happened? Are the girls all right?"

"They're fine. Lauren is studying at a friend's house and the others are in the back yard."

"What's got you looking like you just saw a ghost, then?" Margaret pulled out a chair.

"That's just it." Julie hesitated. "I think I did."

"Did what?"

"You're going to think I'm losing my mind. Maybe I am." Julie drew a deep breath. "I was coming upstairs with an armful of towels and I heard footsteps on the third floor. I knew all the kids were outside, mind you. I went up and glanced in the big room, the one Tansy called the ballroom. And I saw them."

"Saw who, dear?" Margaret asked.

"They were dancing. I saw them. Four couples in clothes like they wore in pioneer days, smiling, dancing, and I heard a fiddler, too. They went around and around and I could see the wallpaper pattern behind them. Or maybe through them."

"What did you do?"

"I watched for a minute, maybe longer, and then I turned and ran down the stairs. It gets worse." Julie dabbed an unbidden tear.

Margaret leaned closer. "Worse? What was it?"

"On the second-floor landing, I bent to pick up the towels I'd left there, and—" Julie shuddered. "—A man brushed by me. He spoke to me, I heard him. "He said, 'Excuse me, Ma'am,' and he bent over and picked up a towel I'd dropped. He held it out to me and said he didn't want to be late."

"What did he look like?"

"Like one of those old guys in the spaghetti westerns, you know, with a checked shirt and a bandana tied at his neck. He smelled like a campfire and horses."

"What did you do?"

"I took the towels from him and ran down the stairs and here I am, wondering if I'm losing my mind." Julie glanced up at Margaret. "Here, smell this towel."

Margaret sniffed. "Smells like clean soap to me, with maybe a hint of woodsmoke and leather. I wouldn't wash it again. Maybe hang it to air out."

"You don't seem particularly shocked."

"Why should I be?" Margaret chuckled. "You know you're not the first to live in Glyth House. Back in the day, that third floor was used by the community. Sounds to me like you ran into a leftover from that time, maybe the shadow of a Saturday night dance. No, I'm not surprised."

"You don't think I'm losing my mind?" Julie asked hopefully.

"I can't speak to that, dear, but it makes sense to me that folks would be dancing in your house. They had a good old time, from what I'm to hear."

"What should I do?" Julie breathed a sigh of relief.

"Well, pour you a glass of milk and have a cinnamon muffin before the children come in, that's what I say. I know your young ones love my muffins." Margaret smiled. "And let the past be where it lays."

Chapter Twenty-One

On the first day of spring, Julie lifted the glass and pulled asparagus spears from the cold frame against the barn. She wondered how long ago that stand had been planted. How many times had she and Tansy picked bright green spears when she was a child? She smiled and bit a raw stalk. Even with half-melted snow drifts in the yard, the glass box was warm enough for asparagus. She glanced at the pea shoots breaking the soil down the rows. Although the Minnesota winter wind still tugged at her scarf, summer would come, as it always did.

At breakfast, Savannah had asked if they could celebrate the equinox "the way we used to, before Daddy left us."

Lauren snapped, "Dad didn't *leave* us. You make it sound like he went on vacation or something. Daddy loved us."

Larkin argued, "He's not here anymore, so he left us."

"It's not like he *wanted* to go," Lauren countered. "You don't understand. You girls are such *children.*"

"We're *supposed* to be children. Mom, isn't that right?" Larkin threw a biscuit at Lauren.

"Mo*ther!*" Lauren thumped the table. "Make these babies stop acting like…babies."

"You stop saying that or I'll tell Mom how you were making eyes at that boy at school," Savannah threatened. "The red-headed one with his nose in a book."

"Okay, knock it off this instant, both of you." Julie waved her fork. "Savannah, celebrating the first day of spring is an excellent idea. We can make some springtime food for lunch and we'll have a dance party to welcome spring. Heaven knows it's been a long enough winter."

Within minutes, a plan was in place. Julie would make hot cross buns, a quiche, and pasta salad, Savannah agreed to bake a lemon cake, Larkin and Holly would help Lauren push back the furniture in the front room for dancing. Lauren offered to help the little girls make paper flowers to decorate and come up with a playlist.

"Add in *Here Comes The Sun* by the Beatles, and *The Rose* by Bette Midler. It's not a dance song, but it's a good one and we can play it while we eat," Julie said. "Holly, you can help me grate cheese and cut up vegetables. Bay can crack the eggs for the quiche. You like to stir, right, Bay-baby?" She consulted her cell phone's screen. "Springtime officially begins at 12:27 this afternoon, so we don't have much time."

The morning passed quickly. The front room took on a party air with the tissue flowers and cake on display, the rugs rolled up and the furniture pushed back. Lauren had made a poster reading "Welcome

Spring!" Larkin had penciled over it, "Go Away, Winter."

Julie debating telling Holly and Larkin to put on something warmer than their swimsuits, then decided they were entitled to welcome the season however they saw fit. She ran up and slipped on a breezy flowered sundress with spaghetti straps. "Can't beat 'em, may as well join 'em." She rubbed her arms against the chill.

Music wafted up the staircase. Savannah came out of her bedroom wearing shorts and a red striped tank top. She picked up three-year-old Bay and hurried downstairs. "We're going to a dance party! See, Lauren's wearing her little ruffled skirt."

Too little; Julie made a mental note to discourage her eldest from wearing that skirt in public.

"Dance, dance," Bay repeated, patting her glittery headband. "We're gonna dance."

"I'm amazed she ever learned to walk down stairs, the way you girls carry her down every time." Julie paused on the landing, smiling at her daughters below. *Those Lazy-Hazy-Crazy Days Of Summer* by Nat King Cole bounced off the ceiling.

"Hurry up, Mommy, look at the clock. Nineteen more minutes of winter!" As Lauren turned up the music, Larkin ran up and pulled Julie's hand.

Holding hands in a circle, they danced, and Julie's heart lifted at the infectious joy in her daughters' faces, their feet flying wildly. One minute before the appointed time, they froze, breathing heavily, eyes on the mantle clock's second hand. As the minute hand moved to 12:27, Larkin shouted, "Ten! Nine!" and the others added their voices to the countdown, ending in a cheer.

"We made it through winter. Bring it on, springtime!"

Lauren cranked up the music. The girls spun and twirled. Bay marched around the room, laughing. Julie caught Larkin and Holly, linking arms in an impromptu cancan line. Savannah and Lauren joined the other end. They kicked and kicked until the girls collapsed in breathless laughter on the floor.

"Whew, ladies, I'm getting winded." Julie wiped her bangs off her forehead. "How about we stop for some fruit punch?"

"No, Mommy, dance with us!"

"We're not done welcoming springtime!"

"It's tradition!"

Julie grinned, swished her sundress skirt and called, "All right, do-si-do!" She grabbed Lauren's arm then Larkin's. In a moment, they formed a ring, passing hands right over left, left over right, as they'd learned at the town dance last fall. Bay jumped up and down in the center, clapping her hands. The Beach Boy's *Surfin' Safari* wasn't exactly a traditional square dance tune, but the girls' giggles made it oddly appropriate.

Julie reached for Savannah's hand next, but with a hopping sidestep, Savannah suddenly ducked out of the circle with a grin. Julie turned, her eyes on little Bay. The toddler's sundressed hips swung in time to the music, more or less.

Lauren missed a step, stumbled, and grabbed a hand, a hairy, undeniably male hand. Off balance, she jostled Julie, bumping her into Larkin who tripped Holly, who grabbed Savannah's arm and pulled her down to the floor in a tangle of arms and legs.

With a shriek, Lauren dropped the male hand, clicked the music off, and wrapped a lap robe from the couch around her short skirt. "Mother!"

Chapter Twenty-Two

"Josiah?" Julie, suddenly conscious of her bare shoulders, gazed up at two strangers standing next to Josiah. "Who is this?" The older one's lips twitched under his drooping mustache. The younger one, a red-faced teen, alternately stared at the floor and glanced at Lauren through the hair across his forehead.

"Mother, this is Beck," Lauren stammered. "Beck, my mother. He's in my math class. Beck, what are you doing here?"

Behind him, Josiah held up a hand. "Sorry to interrupt your party, Julie. When I heard the loud music, figured you couldn't hear us knocking at your side door, so we came on in. This here is Jeff Beckett, the feller I told you about, come to see about putting in a retaining wall." He cast a sidelong glance at Jeff. "And his nephew, goes by Beck. Seems Beck likes to dance."

"Uh, oh, yes, I remember. I wasn't expecting anyone to drop by." Red-faced, Julie swiped her hair from her face. "Clearly."

"Hope I'm not intruding, Mrs McCain. I just finished up a job of work over Edison way, and Josiah here said I might could be of use to you." Jeff's blue eyes skimmed the girls, all frozen in place. "Lovely ladies, what's the occasion?"

Savannah, Larkin, and Holly stared at him, silent, until he turned away, his face flushed.

"The retaining wall? Oh." Julie smoothed her skirt. "We're, uh…"

"Celebwating spwing!" Bay held up her arms to Jeff.

"Celebrating spring? I've never thought to do that." Jeff Beckett grinned at Bay and glanced out the window. "With the winter we've had, it's a mighty fine idea. We can come back another time…"

"No, this is okay," Julie rubbed her bare arms. "Give me a chance to put on some warmer clothes and I'll show you where the slope is coming down. I think we need a stone wall." As she headed for the stairs, she heard Larkin invited Jeff, Beck, and Josiah to join them for lunch. Lauren bolted past her without a word. Julie sighed. That look…*oh, it begins.*

A few minutes later, Julie came down the stairs in jeans and a sweater, her hair in a ponytail. Lauren was already downstairs, dressed in jeans, pouring punch for everyone. She'd taken time to smooth her hair, Julie noted, but her face still burned red.

Jeff grinned at Julie. "With your hair up like that, you look like one of your daughters."

Flustered, Julie cleared her throat and headed for the coat closet. "Come on, then. Girls, set three more plates for lunch. We won't be long."

Josiah trailed across the yard behind Julie and Jeff. Margaret had scolded him over supper last night for saying he thought Julie needed a life of her own. "Don't you think she has enough on her mind, without some man barging in? She's just now getting her feet under her."

"Her husband's been gone over a year, and she's still a young woman." Josiah defended himself. "Hate to think of her raising those young ones by herself, then spending the rest of her days alone. Julie's too alive for that, to my mind. She needs some interest of her own."

"Some romantic interest, you mean? With that batch of girls keeping her on her toes, when would she have time for that, old man?"

"A little bit of romance never hurt a woman," he said, stubbornly. "Look what it's done for you, sweetheart."

"Oh, you." She playfully swatted him with her napkin. "There'll be plenty of romance in that household soon enough, what with Lauren at that age and her sisters not far behind. Don't you go match-making."

When he saw the Beckett brothers' truck parked down the way later that morning, an idea grew in Josiah's mind. Since Jeff Beckett's wife had died in that boating accident some years past, Josiah had seen a haunted look in Jeff's eyes. He'd heard Jeff had taken to drinking, but a man grieved in his own way. Julie had mentioned she was thinking about having a retaining wall built in the side yard. While Josiah enjoyed helping her family, he knew his days of laying heavy rocks were past. He strolled down to talk to Jeff Beckett and his brother, Ben.

They heard the old man out, and Jeff said they'd have time next Monday to take a look at the slope. Ben grinned at Josiah; he'd also been aware of the new family in the Glyth House, including their pretty mother, and he knew his brother was lonely.

"Run along with Josiah," Ben urged, "and take young Beck here with you. You don't need my input. You could build a rock wall in your sleep."

Jeff surveyed the slope and agreed it needed help before the ground gave way. "Looks like about $1450 in materials if you want plain river rocks, more if you go for something fancy."

"Oh, that's less than I thought. How much for stacked grey stones like the fence in the front yard?" Julie led him to the side of the house and pointed. Josiah sat on a bench, letting them go on without him.

"Closer to $1675, I'd guess," Jeff said.

"And labor?" Julie did some quick calculations in her mind.

"About…Look, this won't take me more than a couple of days if the weather cooperates. Tell you, what, Mrs McCain. Make you a deal. Flat eight hundred, including materials, if you'll go out to dinner with me."

Josiah grinned from his perch, unable to hear their words, but pretty sure Jeff was smart enough to see an opportunity when she was standing in front of him, hair in a ponytail.

"Dinner? Me?" Julie froze in her steps. "Like a date? I—"

"I'm thinking about that seafood place over in Madsen Heights. Best Northern Pike anywhere. Of course, we'd have to be on a closer basis, first names, maybe." Jeff pulled his glove off and extended his hand. "Nice to meet you. I'm Jeff. And you are…?" He took her mittened hand.

"Julie. I'm Julie. Dinner would be very nice." She looked up into his eyes with a smile. "I admit it's been a while since I've been on a date."

"Same for me." His eyes warm, he dropped her hand. "Don't look now, Julie, but there's a row of very interested eyes in your window and another pair peeping from behind the curtain. How about we take pity on poor Josiah, who must be cold by now, and head on in? I saw a cake with flowers on it. We'd best get in there before my nephew demolishes it. This age, can't fill a boy up."

Chapter Twenty-Three

It feels so strange to have a dinner date, Dan. You're the only one I've wanted to be with since we first met. I want you to know, though, that this is just dinner, no romance or any of that stuff. He gave me a steep discount on the retaining wall, and one dinner won't hurt anybody. I still love you best, and I always will; don't worry about that.

She pulled her sock up and smiled. *You would have loved the welcome spring party, Dan. The kids danced and laughed like they did every year when you were here. And you should have heard the girls once Jeff and his nephew left. Josiah, that scoundrel, didn't stay for lunch, said his mason bees needed attention. While we cleaned up from the party and lunch, Savannah was the only one without a nice thing to say. She said Beck Beckett's name sounded like a speech impediment, like he's stammering. Lauren lit into her like she'd kicked a kitten. I saw how Lauren looked at him, that bright-eyed first-crush expression. Doomed, I fear."*

Speaking of romance, Larkin reported Savannah's been swooning over a boy at school, some kid named James. Savannah swatted her with a dishtowel. Swooning, she said; guess I need to keep a tighter rein on her reading material, if she sees romance around every corner. I know it's just a matter of time before they all figure out that boys are not just grimy-fingered mouth-breathers. Like your dad says, a boy is a heap of noise with a lot of dirt on it. True, when they're little, but I know there'll come a time when boys will be very interesting to our daughters.

Dan, I wish you were here to help guide them. I know a lot about girls, but what do I know about how a young man thinks? She smiled slowly. *Okay, okay, I do know how you thought, and that's exactly what I'm worried about. Meanwhile, don't give my Friday night supper with Jeff Beckett another thought. Life is too busy for thinking about any romance, and there's no way he could measure up to you anyway. I was blessed to have an awesome love life with you. It'd be greedy to ask for more.*

Julie pulled the hem on her plaid blouse straight and smoothed her hair. *Ridiculous,* she muttered under her breath. *It's just dinner.* She headed downstairs to check on supper for the girls.

Although the week had been as busy as usual, Friday night had been on her mind all week. Jeff had met her at the stone supply store outside of town on Wednesday. He approved her choice of smooth grey stones for the retaining wall's facing and added in cement blocks for the main section that would hold up the slope. With spring rains saturating the earth, he hadn't been able to start work, but promised he and his nephew would be there early Saturday if the forecast held.

Lauren cast an appraising eye at her mother as Julie entered the kitchen. She set down the spoon. "Really, Mother, plaid on a first date?"

"It's just supper, not a date." Julie tasted the stew. "More oregano, I think."

"Well, if you want to know what I think, I think Jeff is too young for you. He can't be a day over forty. What would Dad think of you running around town with another man?"

"What are you talking about? I'm not forty, myself, you know." Julie caught Lauren's hand. "Come sit down. You know your Dad loved me, loved you all. I'm not looking to replace him. I'm just going to dinner. But I'm not dead yet, and if I find someone to love, you girls may have to deal with it. Just as when you find someone special, I will support you *if* he's the right guy." She held up her hand. "No great rush, mind you; you need to get your education first. You'll be graduated and off to college before we know it. As for me, it's just one meal together. Beck said this place has good Northern Pike and you know I like fish."

Lauren hugged Julie. "Well, if you're not going for romance, that awful plaid shirt is perfect."

"Fine, I'll go change."

Chapter Twenty-Four

The next morning, Julie peeked out the window. Sure enough, Margaret's kitchen window cast a warm glow on the dark grass, as good as a welcome sign. She scrawled a note and left it on the table. "Be right back. Stay put," although she expected she'd be back long before any of the girls woke up. She grabbed a cardigan on her way out, tugging the sleeves over her arms as she crossed the grass and walked through the gate.

"Margaret?" She tapped on the door. "It's me, Julie. Can I come in?"

"You're up early. Come on in." Josiah opened the door, blotting his mustache. "All well at your place? Have you had your breakfast?"

"Good morn—" Margaret turned from the stove, spatula in hand. "Uh, oh, Josiah, you'd best go check on the laying hens. Run along."

"I'm eating my hot cakes—" he protested, then took a closer look at Julie's face. "The hens can wait, but I believe I'll eat my breakfast in the front room today. The light's better there." Nodding at his wife, he gathered his plate and the morning newspaper and left.

"Come sit right down, dear. Are you unwell? Shall I make some chamomile tea to settle your stomach?" Margaret turned off the stove burner and moved to the table.

"Chamomile tea? That's the last thing I want. Aunt Tansy always made me drink it when I felt sick, and it's horrible stuff." Julie sagged into a straight-back chair. "My stomach's upset, all right, but tea won't help."

"Some food then? It's mighty early. Have you eaten yet?"

"No, thanks. I can still feel my dinner, sitting in my middle like one of the retaining wall rocks." Julie put her face in her hands. "Oh, Margaret, I'm such a fool."

"Now, things can't be as bad as all that." Margaret settled across the table. "Tell me all about it, if you'd like."

Julie told Margaret Jeff had invited her to dinner. Margaret made a mental note; that old man of hers hadn't listened and now Julie was upset. She'd have words with Josiah later.

"Yes, supper, go on," she urged.

"Well, Jeff was right about the restaurant," Julie said slowly. "I ordered the pike and it was delicious."

"Unless the fish was gone bad, that's not what has your eyes so red this morning, is it?" Margaret patted the younger woman's hand. "Get it all out, dear. It'll be less inside you, festering, once the words reach the light of day. I've heard you tell your young ones that and I know it's true."

In a halting voice, Julie said that halfway through dinner, Jeff Beckett admitted the reason he'd

taken the job of building a retaining wall at Glyth
House was to get a better look at the place. "I think
he'd been drinking; letting his mouth run away with
him. He said he had no need of such a puny job when
he had plenty of other work to keep him busy. He'd
always wondered how far back the property went.
Figured putting in the wall would give him a chance to
walk the survey lines. Planned to talk me into
subdividing it, letting him build some of those tract
houses on the river side of it. He said he could make a
killing on it and we could split the profits."

"Split profits on *your* place?" Margaret
gaped. "That man has always been a scallywag,
looking to make a dime without a lick of work. I
remember Tansy sending him packing once she caught
him with his measuring tape in her front room when
she'd stepped out to get a book he'd come to borrow.
Borrow? No, he had his eye on turning Glyth House
into some kind of conference center, that's what he
told Tansy, knock down every wall inside the old
house. Imagine such a thing? And in Wilsonville!" She
sniffed. "What did you do last night when he said
that?"

"I didn't know what to say. I felt like
somebody punched me in the stomach. I love Glyth
House! I stood up and walked out before dessert was
served. I feel so foolish. Here I thought he just wanted
to build my retaining wall, gave me a good price to be
neighborly."

Tears flooded Julie's eyes. "And to think I wore my good blue blouse. Why didn't I see through him?"

"Now, you go ahead and cry if you need to," Margaret said. "But I won't have you thinking you did anything wrong. You have a good heart and you're not the kind to go looking for ill in people. That man is a snake, no two ways about it, and the Good Lord forgive me for saying it."

"What am I going to do?" Julie wiped her eyes. "I still need the wall built, but I can't let anyone put Glyth House at risk."

"I'd recommend that other Beck, his brother, his name is Benjamin. Smart as a whip and trustworthy, too. Him and his boy, the one in school, they'd be the ones to build your wall. You give him a call."

"Jeff's nephew? I think we met." Julie choked a sob back and giggled. "From what I could see, he and Lauren have more than math on their minds."

"You poor dear, you do have your hands full. A break would do you good. Are you free sometime this week to go see the new shipment of flowers at the big nursery over in Ableville? I'd appreciate the company."

Margaret smiled. "I'd offer you some breakfast now that you're calmer, but I see your kitchen lights just turned on."

"Another day begins." Julie stood and hugged Margaret. "Thanks for letting me talk. And yes, the nursery sounds good."

"Anytime, dear." As soon as the door shut behind Julie, she called, "Josiah? Josiah, let me tell you what your meddling did. I told you, old man…"

Chapter Twenty-Five

Benjamin Beckett knocked on Julie's door that afternoon. "Josiah called me this morning. I'm sorry to hear what my brother said. Jeff's always been one to put money ahead of what's right. More so, now that he's taken to drinking on more than weekends. How about I put up the retaining wall for you? You already have the materials, and I'll charge you a fair price for labor. Okay with you if my son helps out?"

They shook on the deal and the wall was begun in short order. Lauren found one excuse after another to be out there with Beck and Ben for the first day, then gave up and simply volunteered to help after that.

Before long, having Beck at the house was as natural as Margaret dropping in. He lingered after walking Lauren home from school most days. Lauren insisted they were just study-buddies, but it seemed to Julie that they spent a lot more time making snacks in the kitchen and laughing together than cracking the books. She refrained from nagging: Lauren was already at the top of her class and Beck not far behind.

"Mother, do you have a minute to talk?" Lauren settled into the chair across from Julie. "I waited until the little girls were occupied."

"Sure, what's on your mind?" Julie bit the thread off and set Bay's rompers aside. With the children growing so fast, she rarely saw the bottom of the mending basket.

"Well, you see, I was just wondering…" Lauren hesitated. "It's just that, you really loved Daddy, didn't you?"

"Of course, I did. I loved him like my own soul." Was Lauren missing her dad more than usual?

"The thing is…How did you know he was the one?" She hesitated. "How will I know if the man I marry is a good man? I want somebody to love me like Daddy loved you."

"It's good that you're thinking about this now, instead of waiting until some cute boy turns your head, daughter." Julie considered. "How about if you make a list? You know, of traits you really value, and of deal-breakers. That way, any boy you like, you can measure against your list, before you get distracted by his long eyelashes or something."

"That's a good idea. Can I sit here by you while I write?"

"Of course." Julie rethreaded her needle as Lauren bowed her head over a spiral notebook. They worked in silence.

Finally, Julie asked, "I'm curious. What do you have so far?"

"Well, I know you'd tell me not to look on the outward appearance, like the Bible says, but really, he'd have to be decent looking."

Julie nodded. "Go on."

"He has to know God. I want to raise my children in faith so that's a deal-breaker. And he has to be mature and know how to work, not like some of those boys at school. Honestly, Mother, they're pathetic drips and if they have a brain in their heads, there's no evidence."

"Strong language." Julie grinned. "What else?"

"He has to be kind; that's important to me. I mean, a boy who makes fun of a disabled kid or one who kicks puppies could turn out to be a killer. Or even a politician, you know?"

Julie glanced at Lauren's solemn face and suppressed her smile. "You're listing good traits. You want to figure out what really matters to you, versus what's fleeting."

"And he'd have to be crazy about me. I've been watching the way Josiah treats Margaret. I asked him one time why he stands up every time she walks into the room. You know what he told me? He said, 'She's like a queen to me, and queens deserve respect.' Isn't that just dreamy?"

Before Julie could respond, Lauren continued. "I remember Daddy always carrying shopping bags and things for you, doing little things to make your life easier. I want that kind of a husband."

"Sounds to me like you're on the right track. Maybe you can keep that list and add to it as you think about more traits." Julie wagged a finger teasingly.

"And don't forget, you need to be the kind of woman a man like that wants to marry."

"I will, Mother. Can you tell me again how you two met?"

Savannah's voice came from the kitchen. "Wait, I want to hear the story, too, now that you guys are done being sappy."

"You were listening in?" Lauren swatted her sister, then moved over to make room for her. "Tell us."

"You already know this story, girls."

"Tell us again," Lauren ordered. "You were in an art class at college…"

"It was a ceramics class, a pottery class, actually, not the kind with molds." Julie smiled. "And on the third day, I noticed a cute young man watching my hands while I threw a bowl on the potter's wheel. Not me, just my hands, and he was so intent on them, I was able to check him out and he didn't notice. Red hair with waves you could surf on, those gemstone-blue eyes with the copper flecks…You know your dad."

"And then he said—" Savannah prompted.

"And then he said I had beautiful hands and his face turned red, right to his ears. He admitted he'd mastered a pinch pot, but however did I manage to center clay on the potter's wheel?" Julie smiled. "He was a romantic, you know, and he played that selective incompetence card whenever he could get away with it."

"What's that, Mommy?" Larkin shut the door behind her and sat beside Julie. "Are you telling about Daddy?"

"Yes, and you know what she means," Lauren said. "If Dad pretended not to know how to do something, Mother would show him how."

"And it usually ended in a kiss," Savannah added. "Now, hush, Mom's getting to the good part."

Julie chuckled. "In this case, I had Dan sit at the wheel, and I showed him how to hold his hands. I told him he needed to use his fingers like tools when he centered clay, not let it get the better of him. We both got clay to our wrists—he was messy—but he ended up with a pot about four inches tall."

"And then…"

"And then he invited me out for an Italian soda after we cleaned up and we discovered we both liked the same flavor." Julie sighed dramatically, her hand to her brow. "And then we married and had five beautiful daughters who need to go get dinner started."

"Oh, Mother!"

Dan, you'd be so proud of Lauren. Can you see the list she came up with? Hard worker, kind, smart, educated, devoted, enthusiastic…She described her daddy.

Chapter Twenty-Six

Julie swallowed a yawn and reached for another handful of crisp beans.

"You feeling alright, dear?" Margaret eyed her. "You're yawning a lot today."

"I'm okay, thanks, just tired. Holly's been having nightmares, waking up screaming every night. Nobody's getting much sleep in our house." She covered another yawn. "I admit I'm starting to worry about her."

"Is that it? Poor little mite. Does she say what's bothering her?

"She has some imagination. She says she's hearing things, music, footsteps, whistling. You know how it is; once we're asleep, our subconscious can run amok. That's all it is." She called, "Larkin, mind you stay between the rows."

"You have fine daughters, and I surely appreciate your help. Once we get all these beans blanched and in the freezer, we'll have us a nice lunch under the trees. And of course, I'll send a good bit home for your freezer, too."

Julie demurred, "Oh, you don't have to—"

"Well, that was my aim, so there. More here than Josiah and me could eat in a year's time. Now, about your little one. Is it possible she's not imagining things?"

"What do you mean?"

"Well, when you walk into a room , you bring your shadow with you, right? What if those who lived in Glyth House before you left a bit of their shadow behind them, in a way?"

"Wait." Julie knit her brows. "Are you saying Glyth House is haunted? My daughter's seeing ghosts?"

"Not saying a thing for sure and certain, mind you, but Holly's not the first to hear things others can't over there. Dancing on the upper floor, voices in the hallway." Margaret called, "That's wonderful, girls, you saved me a week's worth of work and I thank you. Let's go inside and get the beans into boiling water, then we'll make a picnic lunch while they cool enough to pack for the freezer. Too pretty a day to eat indoors."

Julie stared at the older woman as she cheerfully herded the girls into her kitchen, as calmly as if she'd stated today was Tuesday, not their home had ghosts.

Chapter Twenty-Seven

The following Tuesday afternoon, Julie looked up from her lap top at the kitchen table. She blinked. What had distracted her from paying the bills online? Bay was napping on Margaret's daybed; she'd fallen asleep an hour ago while Margaret showed Julie some vintage embroidered handkerchiefs, and the old woman said she'd bring the child back after her nap. Lauren was doing a job-study day at the clinic, and Larkin and Holly wouldn't be home from school for a couple of hours. She stretched her arms over her head and yawned. Bills took more mental energy than she wanted to exert on a sunny afternoon and her mind felt foggy. If only Holly slept better…why, last night was the first she'd slept through without waking up hollering over a bad dream. Worse than Bay, who at least slept through the night most of the time.

She heard it again, soft tinny notes. The tinkling music came again from the front room. As Julie moved from the kitchen, she heard it again; seven clear notes.

Da-DA-da-dee-dee-da-DA.

She scanned the room; none of the girls had a music box. What could it be? She checked her cell phone on the side table, although the sound was unfamiliar, not a normal ring tone. She stood with her hands in her pockets. Dust motes danced in a shaft of sunlight, the specks twirling like tiny dancers. The notes played again, distinct but tinny, like one of

Margaret's music boxes. Had Bay carried one home
from her last visit? Julie paused, waiting for the notes
to sound again and was not disappointed. She listened
and followed the sound toward the chaise lounge. In
front of the bow windows, it was one of Holly's
favorite reading spots. She shook out Holly's sweater
then draped it over the back of the seat.

Julie sat back on the lounge, puzzled. There
was no hiding place on the chair or underneath it.
Where was the music coming from? She waited,
waited, but the room stood silent. She closed her eyes
to listen better. Julie dozed and dreamed. In her mind,
the dust motes morphed into dancers, their feet light on
the wind, moving in time to the notes she'd heard
playing softly. *Da-DA-da-dee-dee-da-DA,* over and
over.

Julie gasped at a bang. The music faded as
she leaped to her feet. Disoriented, she reeled, then
shook herself. *The door.* It was just the door. She
hurried across the floor, the dancing dust swirling in
her wake.

Someone knocked again then called, "Julie,
are you in there? Julie? The door is stuck shut."

Guiltily, Julie pulled it open. "Sorry,
Margaret, I can't seem to shake the habit of locking the
door. Too long in the city, I'm afraid. Bay, honey, did
you have a nice nap?"

"Apple." Bay held up a handful of apple
wedges.

"She slept like a little angel, and woke up happy," Margaret reported. "You have lines on your cheek, dear. Did you press up against something?"

Julie's hand flew to her face. "Oh! It's from Holly's sweater. I must have dozed off. I came in to find a...sound, and the sunshine felt so good."

"You found a what, dear?"

"You'll think I'm losing my mind." Julie's face reddened. "I thought I heard a music box."

"Not a thing out of sort with that."

"Except we don't own any music boxes."

"Elizabeth collected them. You might be hearing one of hers." A smile played around Margaret's lips. "Bay, dearie, go wash your hands in the bathroom, will you? Apples are sticky."

Julie frowned. "Who's Elizabeth?"

"Why, she was Tansy's mother. A bit eccentric, not a loving woman, I'm given to hear, but I can't say I ever met her."

"She'd be over 150 years old by now. Do you think one of her music boxes could still be here in the house after so many people coming and going?" Julie walked to the lounge chair. "It sounded like it was coming from over here, but I couldn't find anything."

"That makes sense to my mind. I recall shelves above the window some years back. Tansy wasn't a one for music boxes and gave them all away when she had the room repainted. Why, that one Bay likes to play with was one of Elizabeth's."

"You're letting my toddler play with an antique?"

"How will she learn to take care if we keep her from things that need caring for?" Margaret asked, "That old photo album Tansy kept…where is it, dear?"

"In the piano bench. I didn't want Bay pulling the pictures out. She's pretty rough with books." Julie returned with the thick album.

Margaret sat on the sofa and slowly turned the book's pages. "My, what memories! Look here, there's a Sunday School picnic on the lawn, and would you look at the hats the ladies wore? Oh, my, there's old George Wilson himself, the one with the big pocket watch fob on his belly. And his wife, a mousy little woman, I've heard tell."

Julie sat beside her and soon she was engrossed in the daguerreotypes. "Look, there's a whole crowd on Glyth House steps. How did they walk in those skirts?"

"Ah, yes, you found the one I was hunting after. That older woman, the one in the rocking chair, that's Elizabeth. Tansy was just a mite. That's her sitting on the top step below Elizabeth."

"Oh, and she's the one with music boxes? Elizabeth had a solid face, sturdy. I can see that even though nobody else is smiling in this picture, either."

"It's not like nowadays when folks run around with cameras and those little phones in their pockets. Why, I saw your Savannah sneaking up on a black beetle with her phone camera, as if anybody needed a picture of a bug." Margaret shrugged. "Back then, photographers told people not to smile. They'd have to hold right still for a while and smiles are harder to hold steady than a relaxed face. That's why everyone looks so solemn." She pointed to a baby on the left side of the photo. "And why those who wiggled looked blurry. This youngster looks like his legs fell plumb off. Yes, you're right, Elizabeth was a good woman, from all I've heard, raised fourteen fine children. Tansy was her youngest, and took after her. See the resemblance?"

"Fourteen?" Julie glanced out the window. "Oh, it's that late already? The girls are coming up the walk."

Holly ran ahead and burst through the door ahead of her sisters. "Mommy? Mom, look at the book Teacher gave me."

Savannah smiled at Julie and dropped her backpack. "My brain is melted. I'm putting off tackling that science paper until the weekend."

Larkin shut the door behind her. "Mom, can I have a muffin? What's for supper?"

"At least say hello to Margaret. You girls are like a tornado." Julie smiled. "How was your day?"

Larkin told about her killer math test and Savannah described her costume for the upcoming all-school play. Bay climbed onto Julie's lap. Lauren came in, and the girls' voices swirled.

"Mother, I got to stay at the clinic all day. Dr Simms let me practice sutures on a rag doll, and he said I have a real skill at it. Thanks to Margaret—all that handwork paid off! Did you know most incisions are closed with a plain old blanket stitch?"

"It was times tables and I hate times tables, but that verse Josiah taught me made the nines stick in my head. I got 100% on the math test."

"Teacher said I can move into the next reading group after I finish this book. It's about a mouse at the circus, see?" Holly sat beside Margaret. "What book is this? It looks old."

"Fish for supper, and I made a peach pie for dessert. Good work on the test, Larkin, and you can tackle your homework later, Savannah. Rest your minds a bit." Julie focused on Holly. "That's a book of people who lived around here long ago." She paused. "Honey, what is it?"

"See, Mommy, that's her." Holly eagerly pushed the book toward her mother, grinning. "That's the woman who sang to me. In this picture, the one with the apron on. I know her."

"What woman?" Julie glanced at the photo. "You don't know her. That picture was taken a very long time ago."

"I told you this morning. I had a bad dream last night and a nice woman sat on my bed and sang to me. She said not to be afraid. Her name is Miss Ellie and she said Glyth House was a good place for little girls to grow up. She told me there's a little door in my closet with books I can read. Then she sang me a song and I fell asleep and I didn't have a bad dream anymore."

Da-DA-da-dee-dee-da-DA.

The girls fell silent as seven clear notes sounded in the room.

Holly jumped up. "That's it! That's how the song started."

Everyone stared at Holly.

"Mother, where did that music come from?" Lauren edged closer to Julie.

"What's the matter with you all?" Holly stared at her sisters, two bright spots on her cheeks.

Margaret sang softly.

*"When the wind in the reeds blows
soft in the night,
children are tucked in their
beds safe and tight.
As the night creatures stir,
and the fishes swim deep
the young ones sleep safe until sun up,
the Good Lord will keep."*

Da-DA-da-dee-dee-da-DA

When the sun slips below clouds of pink and gold,

*The moon rises in the dark sky so bold
the young ones sleep until dawn sun comes again,*

And the Good Lord keeps watch over his children."

As Margaret finished her quiet song, the music box notes sounded again.

Da-DA-da-dee-dee-da-DA

Holly clapped her hands. "That's *it!* How did you know that song? That's the one Miss Ellie sang to me."

Margaret gathered Holly into her arms, meeting Julie's startled gaze over the child's tousled head. "Oh, I learned that a very long time ago. Your mama's aunt Tansy taught it to me, and her mother taught it to her. I used to sing it to my young ones when they had trouble sleeping. And they never had a bad dream again." She cupped Holly's face. "And now that *you* know the song, you won't have any more bad dreams either."

"No, I won't, not ever again. That's what Miss Ellie said, too. And she said big girls don't cry in the night." Holly nodded, locking eyes with Margaret.

"Girls, why don't you go play. We'll have supper in a couple of hours." Julie herded the girls toward the kitchen door.

"Margaret, what do I do now?" Julie asked when she returned. "We can't very well live in a house with its own ghost!"

"And why not, I'd like to know? It was her home first, and clearly, Miss Ellie wants you here. It won't do any harm for young Holly to be sung to sleep once in a while."

"But by a *ghost?*"

"Really, dear, I've never known you to be judgmental." Margaret sniffed. "I happen to know Miss Ellie kept your aunt company many a lonesome winter's day. You know Tansy cared for her in her old age, right in this very house."

"Tansy never told me about a ghost!"

"Tansy never told you a few things, I'd bet my best hat. Did you ever ask why she hadn't a family of her own?"

Chapter Twenty-Eight

"Well, yes, I did. And Tansy's story stuck with me." Julie settled in for a story. "I was sixteen that summer when Mom and Dad were off on another of their trips, some safari or something, I don't know. They left me with Tansy at Glyth House. You know how sixteen-year-olds are; inquisitive is the polite term, but nosy is more like it. One afternoon, I asked Tansy why she never married. I knew all my friends had families and I certainly dreamed of my own someday. I think Tansy was the only adult I knew who was single her whole life, and definitely the only one I'd have dared ask.

"Shoo, girl, nobody cares about an old lady." Tansy brushed my blunt question aside. "Tell me about your classes next term. Goin' on with your artwork, are you? You have a deft hand with paint, better than some museum displays, to my mind."

I guess I was feeling extra snoopy that day, and I guess she trusted me enough with her story. I stared Tansy down and she gave me an appraising stare right back, then she finally nodded. "All right, then. I've loved in my day, been loved by a few, but never felt I had enough to give, not enough to make a family of my own and risk them growin' up not feelin' wanted, like I felt."

Tansy not feeling wanted was a foreign concept! Everyone I knew adored her. Well, maybe not my mother so much, but Mom took a dim view of almost everybody and that was true back then, too. I pressed Tansy and she finally told her story.

"You see, girl, I was born too soon. My brother, Thad, was only nine months old at that time, and that may have been part of it; maybe my mother's body was too tired from havin' a new baby to feel happy about another on the way. The way my Papa told me, he took Mama out in the rowboat that late autumn day, thinkin' a rest would do her good, leavin' the care of my older sisters and brothers with her mother, my granny. I don't know if the afternoon relaxed her, but he said when they were nearly back to the dock with a mess of fish, she heard the baby cryin' and didn't wait for him to finish tyin' up the boat. She lost her footin' as she climbed onto the dock, and fell in the cold water, the space between dock and boat. Bein' heavy with child, her balance was none too good. Papa fished her out right off, but within the hour, Mama knew her baby was on the way."

"She must have been excited to meet you."

"Not hardly. My mother was only seven months gone with me when I was born. Nowadays, a too-soon child has a fightin' chance, what with all those newfangled medical things they got, but back then, even a full-sized baby had a slim chance of reachin' adulthood. Granny was a sharp woman, businesslike, not above lashin' out at anyone. She told my Mama not to get her hopes up, this was a baby she couldn't keep; if it was born alive at all, the infant would be too small to live. Anyway, I arrived, and my granny wrapped me in a clean rag. She set me on the hearthstone. Papa said she told him I wouldn't live out the night until mornin', but I may as well be warm as I drew my last breaths."

"That's terrible! A little bitty baby like that. Why didn't they call an ambulance?" I blurted.

"Folks didn't cotton to doctors or hospitals back then except in dire circumstances. A baby bein' born was just part of life, not worthy of a commotion. Mama already had a slew of young ones and a baby in the mix, not even walkin' yet. I guess she was pretty upset when she figured out I was on my way so soon after the last. She made up her mind to not even hold me in case she accidentally loved me, knowin' she couldn't raise me. She just hardened her heart as she birthed me so the loss would hurt less, I guess."

"That's so sad."

"Well, it was. My granny was a practical woman, not a soft bone in her heart, this I know. She told my Mama just to forget the whole thing ever happened. They'd bury the baby the next afternoon."

I wiped a tear. The idea of a tiny baby, unwanted, uncared for hurt my heart. Maybe that's when I decided to love any baby in my future as hard as I could, I don't know. "But, Tansy, we're talking about *you*. You were that baby, and you're not dead. What happened?"

"Well, Papa said Mama cried all night, and all he did was hold her in his arms until she slept at last. A fitful sleep, I'd wager." She shook her head. "As the sun rose, Papa heard me cryin'. He said it sounded like a kitten mewin', but there was a force in it like I was demandin' to be heard. And Papa insisted if I was strong enough to live through the night wrapped in a rag and left on the hearth like a dropped potholder, I was a fighter. He roused Mama and said she had to feed me, tend her baby like any other. Mama turned away, said she wished I was dead. Her heart grew that cold in the night."

"How could that be? You were her baby!"

"Grief is a powerful thing, this I know. In her pain, she decided I was dead and gone and she had trouble turnin' her mind back to motherin' me. Granny told me some years later my Mama said I was the ugliest thing she'd ever seen, all bony and fuzzy like a naked bunny rabbit."

"Your own mother? That had to hurt. What happened next?"

"Papa had words with my granny, once she heard I hadn't died in the night. Seems she believed a baby that small wouldn't live long and why even try to keep it alive. Papa got him some warm milk and fed me himself with a dropper until Mama got over herself enough to tend me."

"Good for him!"

"Yes, indeedy, he was a good man. Men back in those days, they didn't have much to do with the

children or the household, but my Papa loved me.
Mama never did come around to me. She met my
needs, but no more than that. And I expect that's why I
never felt able to have a family of my own. If my own
mother didn't love me, I wasn't worth loving, I
figured."

Julie swallowed hard. "She was wrong, Aunt
Tansy. You have enough love to—to—well, to fill the
sky! You are so good to me and you let us cousins play
with your stuff and make us treats. I know you love
me."

"That I do, Julie, dear. I love you more than I
could have loved you had you been my own young
one. Who knows, maybe I could have been a good
mother…" Tansy stood, brushing off her apron. "Well,
now, we won't never know, will we? I'm a blessed
woman, having you youngsters in my life, I know that.
How about we go see if that apple pie is cool enough
for eatin'?"

Julie stretched her arms above her head. "So,
Margaret, maybe that's what makes me overprotective
of my daughters. I want them to know they're loved, to
have a sure foundation."

Chapter Twenty-Nine

Rain streamed down the windows of Glyth House, and the children's spirits were as muddy as the puddles in the yard.

Julie looked up from her book and sighed. "Can't you girls find something productive to do? All you've done all day is bicker."

"It's not fair, raining on a perfectly good Saturday," Savannah grumbled. "It's been raining for days!"

"Yeah, I want to go outside. Josiah said he'd help us build a tree house, but we can't do anything in this stupid rain." Larkin threw a pillow at Lauren, knocking over Holly's block tower on the way.

Holly let out a howl and Bay joined in. "You broked it!"

"Knock it off, I mean it!" Julie set her book aside and hugged the littlest girls. "Let's plan something fun to do once the rain lets up."

"It's *never* going to stop," Lauren broke her pencil point and growled. "The roads are so bad, Beck can't even ride his bike over."

"Boys are dumb," Holly contributed, earning her a swat from Lauren.

"Honestly. Lauren, tell your sister you're sorry." Julie sighed. "Holly, boys are not bad things. Daddy was a boy, remember? Who has an idea?"

"Like a day trip? Or camping?" Larkin asked.

"I'm thinking maybe more like a party or a picnic." Julie sat up straighter. "Maybe we could invite some other families to join us."

"Mother, wait. I was looking through this old book yesterday, and it's pretty interesting." Lauren pulled a binder off the bookshelf. "I guess Great-Aunt Tansy liked parties. She kept a running list of what happened at Glyth House, and during the summers, it seemed nonstop. Let me read this to you."

Larkin moved to sit beside Lauren. "I can't read that. What language is it?"

"It's called cursive script," Lauren said. "It's a secret code old people write in."

"Lauren, really?" Julie chuckled. "Larkin, you'll learn cursive in school next fall. I can teach you how to write in cursive this summer if you'd like."

"Yes, I like knowing more than anyone in my class," Larkin nodded. "Read to us, Lauren."

Lauren read, "'May 6, 1919. Planned to go for a long hike now that the snow is mostly gone. Invited a few others. Word spread. 68 townsfolk climbed White Ridge. Cooked hot dogs on a fire later on. Good to see friends after a long winter. Not one lost.'"

"A hike sounds like fun," Savannah said. "But would people come?"

Lauren ignored her. "'July 22, 1936. Community picnic at Glyth House. 77 in attendance.

Plenty of food. Croquet and badminton and men played horseshoes. After supper, men laid a floor. Fiddlers. Danced far past midnight. Great success.' And this one. 'August 1963. Sunday School supper. Preacher Moss spoke for a mercifully short time, children played, good food. Grateful for good friends.'" Lauren skipped a few pages. "'Cleaned the cemetery for Decoration Day, picnic lunch followed. Good for the youngsters to be taught. E.M. still refuses to share her sour pickle recipe. Good day otherwise.'" Lauren set the book aside. "It doesn't say who E.M. was. There are years of ideas here. And she ended every entry with something positive."

"Let me look." Julie reached for the binder. "There was always something going on here when I visited when I was your age, and I remember Tansy writing in this same book. " She thumbed through the pages. "Look at this. Dance parties on the third floor, game nights, taffy pulls, covered dish suppers. It just goes on."

"Tansy sounds like she loved people," Savannah remarked.

"Oh, she did! And any excuse to get people together, too, that was her way." Julie smiled. "Why, she could even make work sounds like fun. I remember the apple harvest. Back then, people preserved apples by drying them, and it was a chore, preparing them. She'd invite young people to come to the barn and they'd peel bushels of baskets of apples, cut slices and string them up to dry. It took hours."

"That doesn't sound like fun." Holly wrinkled her nose. "That sounds like work."

"You didn't know Tansy! Yes, they worked, but the teens had a chance to talk and even flirt a bit." Julie smiled. "After the work was done, Tansy would serve warm apple crumble, and somebody would start some games. Those afternoons were so much fun. Glyth House was a center of the community, mostly because of Tansy. What do you think she'd say if she saw us all droopy on a rainy afternoon?"

Larkin offered, "She'd say 'Bring me some apples to peel.'"

When the laughter died down, Julie said, "Girls, Glyth House is our home now. Let's plan something fun, something that will let us meet the rest of the people who live around here. Larkin, pass me that tablet, will you? Tell me your ideas."

Within a few minutes, they'd filled six sheets of paper with proposals. Julie set her pen down. "Wow, you girls, once you get going, I'm amazed at your creativity. Let's see how we can narrow this down to one day, okay? I don't see how we can do a hike and boating at the same time, but we can do more than one event. We'll have all summer. Let's start with a community picnic, shall we?"

Amid the chatter, Holly ran to answer the door. "Mommy, Margaret and Josiah are here."

"Invite them in. They can help us plan."

Margaret set a basket on the table and pulled her scarf off. "I know rainy Saturdays are no fun.

Maybe some warm raisin cookies might help."

"Raisin cookies? I read about that." Lauren reached for the binder. "Yes, right here. 'May 2, 1977. Rain seems endless. Streets flooding. Josiah and Margaret came over with a new jigsaw puzzle and some of her raisin cookies and saved the day. Good friends.'"

Josiah draped his wet jacket over a kitchen chair and sat down. "That Tansy was a one for writing things down. What are you women up to today?"

Their voices spilling over one another, the plan was soon set forth.

"Oh, my, it will be just like old times. I haven't been to a covered dish supper in ages, and there's something special about eating out of doors." Margaret beamed. "I heard the rain is supposed to break and hold off, so next Saturday should be a fair day. Tell us what we can do to help."

"Maybe some kind of competition," Lauren suggested, "like Tansy wrote about. Do you know what stick-pull is?"

"It's a game boys liked to play," Josiah slapped his leg. "I was pretty good in my day. They'd sit on the ground, legs out in front of them, feet touching, and they'd grab hold of a long sturdy stick. The idea was for one to lift the other off the ground first. That and hoop rolling was part of every get-together for the young ones back in the day."

"Why didn't girls play stick-pull?" Larkin asked.

"It was a different time. Their fancy dresses would get in the way, I suppose." Josiah stroked his mustache. "If you wear play clothes to the picnic, I'll make sure to pair you up with someone your size. We need to finish planning now, but we'll borrow your mama's broom handle and I'll teach you girls how to play before we go."

"I recall the men always liked to have a log-sawing contest at the old picnics, see who could cut through a big log the fastest." Margaret said, "My, I can still hear the whooping and joshing in my mind."

"It would be fun to bring back some of the old games." Savannah asked, "Didn't the women compete, too? You said *men.*"

"Well, things were different back then," Margaret said. "We mostly did our competing though showing off, who could make the fanciest cakes, the best pie, like that."

"I like pie," Bay said, her hand in Josiah's.

"Good idea, Bay. How about a pie-baking competition?" Lauren wrote on the paper. "We'll want dessert anyway."

"Let's ask people to bring an extra pie, a small one, and we can have a pie-*eating* competition, too," Larkin giggled. "That would be funny to watch."

"More fun to be part of it," Savannah chimed in. "We could have different age ranges, for the little kids, school kids, then adults."

"I can't wait. We can put out some lawn games, too." Julie smiled. "What else do we need to plan for?"

Josiah said he'd get some men to help set up sawhorses tables for the potluck supper and make a plywood floor in the front yard, like old times.

"A plywood floor? On the lawn?" Julie raised an eyebrow. "What on earth for?"

"Dancing, of course," Margaret said. "Summer parties always included dancing."

"Oh, I hadn't planned on that. Where will we get music?" Julie said, "Lauren, can you rig up some speakers and download music on your phone?"

"No need of that," Josiah scoffed. "Old man Tom and his fiddling band played at the state fair in St Paul and he's a good friend of my sister's. I'll get him here, you can count on that, and a caller too."

"A what?" Larkin asked. "Call who?"

"You can't have a proper square dance without a caller, now, can you? Leave that to me."

Chapter Thirty

The week was a busy one, what with the girls inviting everyone they knew and telling them to invite others. In Larkin's words, the news spread like wildflowers. People offered to help, including some Julie didn't know. She had no idea how many people would come to the picnic. Fighting anxiety, she took time to read over Tansy's old binder. None of the entries detailed failure, she assured herself. *What could go wrong? I can do this. Probably.*

Saturday dawned bright and clear. Josiah had a crew of men building a plywood dance floor and setting up sawhorse tables before ten o'clock, and another crew hauled in a heap of logs for the sawing competition.

"And we'll have us a log-splitting race, too," one explained, "so you can fit the leftovers in your fireplace next winter. The teens can have a stacking contest, so you won't have to clean up any mess."

By late afternoon, friends and neighbors began to gather. Julie placed the last olives on the salad, drew a deep breath, and pushed open the door.

"Mother, who are all these people?" Savannah asked an hour later as she nestled more soda cans into the ice chest. "I didn't think so many lived around here. Everyone seems so friendly."

"It's more than I expected, but we have plenty of food." Julie snagged a pickle spear. "I think we'd better start eating. We need a prayer. Have you seen Preacher Morgan?"

"He had to go check on something, but he'll be back soon." Josiah was at her elbow. "Want me to offer a blessing on the food? I can do that as well as any old preacher. On second thought, Julie, this is your home now. You do it." Josiah rang the old dinner bell on the side of the house. It took a minute for the group to settle down. They drew near the porch, eyes on Julie.

I'm going to pass out. Julie could see her heart pounding through her striped blouse. She looked at the upturned faces. *I can't speak in front of this many people. Dan always made the speeches.* Until now.

"Everyone, settle down. Julie here is going to ask the Lord's blessing on this food, the bounty you've all provided." Josiah nodded at Julie.

Julie closed her eyes and clasped her shaking hands. "We thank Thee, oh, Lord, for good food and for friends old and new to share it with…" In her mind, Julie saw Tansy beaming at her, urging her on. Her voice strengthened. "Bless us to be a good community and to serve one another. Amen." When the last Amen murmur faded, she called, "Supper's on! Grab a plate, everyone, and thanks so much for coming."

Holly balanced her paper plate on a large rock and sat in the grass. "Mommy, look at all our new friends!"

"It's a good, day, isn't it?" Julie smiled at the sight, dozens of people sprawled on the wide lawn, laughing, talking, eating. "We didn't get to do this in Virginia."

Larkin rubbed her skinned knee. "I won one of the stick pulls, Mom. Did you see me?"

"I sure did. You lifted that boy right off his pockets."

"He was pretty surprised. It's because Josiah taught us girls how to play stick pull in the kitchen last week. The other kids didn't get to practice." Larkin wiped her face. "And I'm going to win the pie-eating contest, too."

"You don't need practice for that," Lauren teased. "I'm not going to play. I don't want whipped cream in my hair in front of everybody."

"Speaking of *everybody*, where did Beck go?" Julie bit her roll. "Who made these? So good!"

"That's the trouble with potlucks; we never get the good recipes." Lauren glanced at her watch. "Beck said he had to go with his dad for a bit, something about his uncle Jeff getting in some kind of trouble. He should be back by now."

"I heard somebody say Jeff Beckett was in jail for shooting out some streetlights in the ballpark." Savannah stood. "We didn't like him anyway. Whole family's crazy, if you ask me." As Lauren reached for her cup, Julie intervened. "Lauren, don't you dare throw that at your sister! Girls, we need to be nice to Mr Beckett. His wife died and he's had a hard time of it."

"Our Daddy died, and you're not shooting at lights," Savannah observed. "I want some more of that potato salad."

"Thanks for not shooting at stuff, Mother." Lauren chuckled, then lowered her voice. "Really, I'm proud of how well you're dealing with Dad being gone. I mean, I know you miss him, but we're doing all right, considering."

Before Julie could react to the unexpected praise, Lauren jumped up, heedless of the plate on her lap. She ran to Beck and he caught her in a hug. After he filled his plate, Julie saw them sitting on the grass, Lauren smiling and talking as he wolfed his supper. She relaxed at last. All was right in her world, and if the noise coming from the wood-cutting competition was any indication, she'd be set for firewood for next winter, too.

Once all the food was put away and the pie eating champs crowned, the notes of a fiddle warming up encouraged people to move to the expansive front yard. Couples took their places, eight to a square, on the wooden dance floor, while others sat on hay bales lining the dance floor Josiah's crew had cobbled together that morning. Overhead strings of lights flashed on, competing with a glorious gold and pink sunset.

"Mom, can I go dance for a bit? Then I'll watch Bay so you can dance, okay?"

Julie waved Savannah off. "Go dance, Honey, we're fine. Have fun." Julie clapped her hands, smiling at Bay beside her. "Savannah's always watching out for us, isn't she?"

"Yook, Mommy, they're dancing." Bay clapped, laughing as the square dance caller led them through intricate dance steps, over under, around, and through.

"Right hands in, left and back, over and under, now do-si-do."

"They sure are." Julie counted her daughters as she did a dozen times every day. Savannah, partnered with a boy from school, kicked up her feet and grinned, moving through the square dance steps as if she'd known them since birth.

Not so Larkin. Holding hands with another little girl, they did their best to keep up and Julie smiled, recognizing the adults' effort to not run them over in the square. Holly stood on a nearby hay bale, dancing in place and clapping. In a different square, Lauren and Beck kept up, grinning at each other the whole time, their hands twining in the right-hand star. Ah, young love, and what could be safer than a community square dance?

Julie took her turn with the perspiring, smiling square dancers a few times. "Josiah, I had no idea what a skilled dancer you are," she said as the caller announced a break, long enough for the lead fiddler to replace a broken string. "I'd better go lay Bay down in her bed. She fell asleep on that hay bale."

"No need, Margaret's got her well in hand."

Margaret carried Bay to a nearby quilt with other sleeping babies and toddlers. She patted Bay's back and came to Julie and Josiah. "Shall we have some more of that fruit punch before the caller drinks it all? I don't know how he keeps his voice, loud as he is. He didn't want a microphone."

People milled around under the lights, smiling, and Julie felt a burble of happiness under her ribs.

The caller shouted for the next dancers to take their places. "Virginia Reel. I know you know this one."

Beck stood in front of Julie and bowed deeply. "May I have this dance, Ms Julie?"

Julie laughed. "Beck, what are you doing?"

"Go on, Mother," Lauren urged. "I'll dance with Larkin. She's having the time of her life, but she's going to trip somebody if we don't rein her in."

Julie checked on Holly's whereabouts and let Beck take her hand as he led her to the wooden dance floor.

"Allemande left, ladies and gents, and ladies' chain to the right, now promenade all." The caller's deep voice kept time with the three fiddlers.

Beck took Julie's arm and led her through back-and-step promenade. *He knows what he's doing, and his hands aren't even sweaty.* Julie laughed as

Beck spun her in a wide circle. It had been too long since she'd relaxed this much. What a great idea, this community party. The only thing missing was Dan.

And then the shots rang out.

Chapter Thirty-One

Julie felt her heart miss a beat, two beats, three, then it slammed against her chest as if making up for lost time. Odd, wasn't it, how crises always happened in slow motion? Beck pushed her to the dance floor, calling Lauren's name. The rhythmic dance steps were replaced by the sound of men's boots thundering across the yard.

A man shouted and another shotgun blast took out the streetlight, then the porch light on the house. The lights lining the driveway were next, one after another. Someone screamed and others shouted. Men ran toward the pick up truck on the road. A baby wailed. Then an eerie silence; was the shooting over?

Julie's breath caught in her throat. "Beck, let go of my arm. I have to—"

"No, Ma'am, not until the menfolk have things in hand. That was a 12-gauge shotgun, I know it. Keep your head down, Ma'am."

A man shouted, "It's mine! Tansy meant it for me, not those outsiders!" and more shots rang out, at least a half dozen shots, but that didn't explain Beck's words. *Ma'am? Menfolk?* Of all times to catapult into the Wild West. Julie squirmed, her face against the rough plywood dance floor. The girls—

"Mommy? Mommy?" Holly cried out. "Mommy, I need you!"

"I've got her, Julie, and Larkin, too." Josiah called, his voice stern. "Stay down, everybody."

Julie couldn't see what was happening by the road, not with Beck pinning her down and the other dancers jumbled around her like pups in a basket, frozen in place. She heard a skirmish, men shouting, and over it all, a slurred shout, "I need this place for my own! I'll take Julie and them kids if I gotta, but Glyth House is *mine!"*

"Aw, Ms Julie, I'm sorry," Beck muttered in her ear. "It's my Uncle Jeff. Sounds like he's got the drink in him again. He goes crazy sometimes. Me and my dad put him to bed, but he sure didn't stay there."

"Not your fault, Beck, every family has one." She reconsidered with a wry smile. "Well, not everybody's crazy family member shoots out lights, I'll grant you that. Oh, finally, I hear a siren."

After a minute or maybe ten, she wasn't sure, a car door slammed and a man bellowed, "It's all over, folks. Sheriff's got Jeff Beckett in the squad car. Everybody all right?"

Slowly the party-goers rose, dusting themselves off. Julie's daughters ran to her, all but Bay, still asleep on the quilt on the grass. Julie buried her face in Larkin's tousled hair, wrapping her arms around her girls, feeling their heartbeats, breathing slowing as their anxiety drained away, drawing strength from them. She squeezed them and released her girls, not noticing until then that Beck was in the circle, as close as any of them.

Ah, well.

Uneasy chatter filled the air as a fiddler tuned his fiddle. The square dance caller wiped his brow and replaced his hat. "Folks, who's in for the next set? We're not gonna let a little night noise break up the party, are we now?"

Chuckling nervously, three squares of dancers took their places on the plywood floor and the music resumed. Others mingled on the grass, talking about what would happen next.

"We'll be back in the morning, Julie, help you replace those shot-out lights."

"I heard tell Jeff's on probation. Sheriff said next trouble he stirs up, he'll land himself in jail."

"He sure stirred it up tonight."

"That drink, that's his trouble. He's a good man when he's sober."

Julie sat on a hay bale, her legs still shaking. Holly cuddled close with her hand on Julie's knee. "Mommy, are we okay? Do we have to go back to Virginia?"

Before Julie could respond, Margaret's firm voice broke the night. "Stuff and nonsense, little one. Your Great-Great-Aunt Tansy loved Glyth House and she wanted your family to live here. Look at all these people, happy to be together. That's because of you. Don't let one crazy man spoil all this."

In the morning, Julie drew the curtains at the sound of pounding. She opened the door and ran down the steps, clutching her cardigan around her. "Josiah, Ben, you're up and about early."

"Thought we'd fix your lights and sweep up the glass before your young ones see it in the light of day. Timothy and his crew will be here soon to take down the dance floor and tables." Josiah grinned. "Some party last night, wasn't it?"

"Finest kind, like old times." Ben twisted a bulb into the new fixture on the pole. "Sorry about my brother, Julie. I went to see him this morning down at the jail. He's got a hangover to beat all hangovers. Told me he's going into one of those residential treatment places up in the city. I guess the sheriff read him the riot act. Said he could have killed somebody last night."

"Good thing he only shoots at lights." Julie sighed. "Rehab will do him good."

"Mommy, can I come outside, too?" Bay stood in the open door in her ruffled nightgown.

"I'll be right there, Bay," Julie called. "Thanks, you guys, for everything."

A while later, as Julie slid bacon and eggs onto a platter, Holly said, "The dance was fun last night, wasn't it? And in the middle of the night, that nice grandma was in my room again, clapping her hands and swishing her skirt. She liked the music, I could tell. You heard the music, didn't you, Mommy?"

Julie dropped the spatula, breakfast forgotten.

Her response was smothered by Bay and Larkin tumbling into the kitchen. "Mama, Larkin called me a female!" Bay wailed. "Make her stop."

"Larkin, stop tormenting your sister, and go tell the girls breakfast is ready. Tell them to hurry or the hash browns will be hash blacks." Julie bit her lip then smiled at Holly. "Honey, can we talk about this later?"

Later that morning, once the only remnants of the picnic were flattened grass and a taller woodpile, Julie opened Tansy's binder and flipped to a fresh page. She wrote,

Community picnic great success. Over 80 people, all had fun. So much good food and dancing past midnight. Holly says dancers were in the house last night, too. Bonus: a new woodpile for next winter. We feel part of the community now. I see why Tansy loved living here.

We are home.

Chapter Thirty-Two

"Do you know what today is?" Julie asked over breakfast. "It's an anniversary."

"The day you married Daddy?" guessed Savannah.

"No."

"America's birthday?" Holly asked.

"No, that's in July, silly." Lauren looked up from her notebook. "What day is it, Mother?"

"It's our family's moving anniversary. We left Virginia exactly a year ago."

"Are we going to celebrate, Mommy? A party?" Larkin grinned.

"I have an idea," Julie said, "a way to let people a long time from now know we lived here. Let's make a time capsule. That way, we can leave our mark on history, and people years from now will know who we are. I found this in the butler's pantry, and I think it's ideal." Julie held up a metal bread box. "Larkin, pass the toast to Bay. We can each put something in the box, something that represents something important to us that happened this past year. Holly and Bay can add a drawing and the rest of us will write a little something about the item we chose. What do you think?"

"Good idea, Mom." Savannah's eyes lit up. "Can we bury it, too?"

Holly asked, "Can I put Hoopy Bear in it?"

"I'm not doing it," Lauren groused. "I need to study."

"I put cookie in box," Bay stated firmly.

Larkin asked, "How will anybody ever find it?"

"Whoa, whoa. One at a time." Julie held up her hand. "Yes, Lauren, you are, we're all going to contribute. Holly, you can't put Hoopy Bear in the box because we're going to dig a hole and bury it and you'd never see your bear again. We can pour cement on top of it, make a marker with the date on it. Maybe your footprints, too. That way, when somebody finds it a long time from now, they'll know it's there. And they'll know we were here. Bay, eat your breakfast and then you may have a cookie. I'll help you find something else to put in the box."

"Where are we going to bury it?" Larkin asked.

"We like spending time by the fire pit, don't we? I thought that might be a good area." Julie added, "We can have some celebratory juice there, too, after we talk about the items you want to add to the box."

Holly high-fived Savannah. "Mine will be best."

"Honestly, you don't have to compete in everything!" Julie scolded. "Let's plan on meeting at the fire pit right after lunch."

As soon as the breakfast dishes were done, the girls scattered. Julie went out to weed the front flowerbed with Bay at her side. "Here, you can dig with the little shovel. Do you know what you want to put in the box yet?"

Bay didn't answer, intent on examining an earthworm. "Mama, worm wiggles."

"Uh, huh." Julie pulled up a chickweed.

"Worm is cold."

"It is?"

A minute later, Bay announced, "Worm broked."

Julie hugged her daughter, feeling Bay's hair warm from the sun against her cheek. If only Dan could see this child! He should be here to love her, to teach her, to explain about worms, even if not all of them survived.

A few hours later, Lauren swallowed the last bite of her sandwich. "Okay, let's get this time capsule over with."

Julie frowned. "Honestly, can't you get onboard with a family project?"

"Oh, I'm onboard, you'll see," Lauren smirked. "Are we ready?"

They picked up their chosen items and Julie grabbed the metal breadbox on their way to the firepit. Once they were settled, she scooped Bay on to her lap.

"I want to go first," Holly said.

"Okay," Julie nodded, "and remember, everybody has to tell about what they're adding to the box. What do you have, Holly?"

"This year, we moved to a new house, an old house. I have this tiny old book. I found it in that little room inside my closet." She held out a four-inch square book with a girl on a swing on the cover. "See, she has a swing like ours. And I drew a picture of me on the swing Josiah hung for us. That way, people will know a little girl lived here."

"Very good, honey." Julie raised an eyebrow. "I didn't know your closet had a room in it, though."

Holly squirmed. "It's a secret, Mommy. It has a little bookshelf, that's all."

"Okay." Julie made a mental note to investigate at another time. "Next?"

"Me!" Larkin unrolled a poster of a moving company truck. "See, this is about when we moved here to Wilsonville. That's important because it's where our family lives now. And my report card. It was a good one."

"I want to go next." Savannah held up a card. "I'm adding a recipe that Margaret gave me for turkey pot pie. This year, we made new friends and you let me cook more. I wrote a little story about that."

"Good, Savannah. Bay, do you want to show what you chose?"

"Okay, Mommy." Bay displayed a drawing that looked like green spaghetti with no plate.

"Tell what it is, honey."

"It's a big-girl bed because I'm not a baby anymore. And this." She dropped a worn pacifier into the metal box.

The others laughed. "That's right, you're a big girl now."

"Lauren, you're next," Julie nodded.

"No, I want to go last."

"All right." Julie said, "I'm adding a copy of Dad's obituary, and a picture of you girls dancing at the town square dance. That tells the story of our loss, but us going on, too. Oh, and this folding marshmallow fork, because we never had a firepit in Virginia and we seem to be cooking a lot of marshmallows since we moved here."

Holly clapped. "Marshmallows!"

Savannah poked Lauren's arm. "What do you have?"

"Well, I'm putting in my trigonometry textbook, because I never want to see it again. It has all my margin notes. In fifty years, somebody will probably wonder what it's good for, but I admit, I wonder that now." Lauren held up another item. "And I'm adding this. It's most important."

They stared at the plastic skeleton in her hand.

"Why is the back of it blue?" Holly ventured, "Is it because we had Halloween?"

"No, silly." Lauren stared at Julie, then averted her eyes. "It's because of Mother."

"Mom's not a skeleton," Larkin giggled. "She has skin and hair and everything."

"She also has a spine. That's what people say when a person is brave, that she has a backbone. We've had a lot of changes this year, and it's hasn't been easy. Have you noticed Mother doesn't cry as much anymore, like she did when Daddy died?"

"Well, she's crying now," Larkin observed.

"I am not," Julie sniveled, holding her arms out. "I love you girls."

Chapter Thirty-Three

Early in the spring of Lauren's senior year, Julie glanced out the window and noticed Lauren lagging behind her sisters after the school van dropped them off at the driveway. "Uh, oh, Bay, looks like Lauren is sad. Can you hug her when she comes in?"

Bay pushed her coloring book aside and ran to the window. "Yes, Mommy, I will make her happy."

Moments later, the door flung open and Savannah, Larkin, and Holly tumbled in, all talking at once. Julie set a plate of cookies on the table and poured milk.

"Mom, it was a killer, but I got a 100% on my algebra test."

"Mommy, the cafeteria had yucky pizza today for lunch. How did they make *pizza* taste bad?"

"Guess what, Mommy? Teacher liked my book report about *The Happy Toads.* We had to read them in front of the whole class, and I wasn't even scared. She said I was a good floo…infloo…"

"Mom, the middle classes are going on a field trip to the planetarium next week. Can you sign this paper so I can go?"

"Okay, okay, one at a time, please!" Lauren smiled, her heart warming with love for her girls. "Good job, Savannah—you studied hard for the test and it paid off. Larkin, sorry about lunch, but we'll have a good dinner tonight. Yes, of course, you may go on the field trip; planetariums are interesting. Savannah, I assume you have the same form for me to sign? Honestly, you and paperwork!"

"Oh, yeah, sorry. Here it is."

Julie scrawled her approval on both papers and handed them back. "Holly, honey, I'm glad you were confident in front of the class, but I'm not surprised. Your teacher probably meant you were a good influence. That means you set an example for the other students. I'm proud of you." She glanced out the window, where Lauren sat on the swing set, her foot scuffing the dirt. "Anybody know what's up with Lauren?"

"I saw Mr Hendricks talking to Lauren outside his office when I went to the library," Savannah volunteered. "He looked really stern and she was wiping her eyes. I asked about it after school and she about bit my head off. I didn't tell her her make-up was smeared."

"That was smart," Julie nodded. "If she was already upset, that would have made things worse."

"Exactly what I figured," Savannah agreed. "Let her take somebody else's head off."

"Lauren must be in biiiig trouble to have to talk to Mr Hendricks." Larkin's eyes were wide. "The school superintendent only talks to bad kids."

"Maybe she got in trouble with Beck." Savannah reached for more milk. "He wasn't at school today."

"Me, me!" Bay pouted, cookie in hand. "All you ever talk about is what did you do in school. Nobody ever asks me!"

"You're right. We get so busy with our own stuff, we forget to ask about how your day went." Savannah hugged Bay. "So, Bay, what did you and Mommy do today?"

Bay's eyes lit up. "We went to a farm and we saw a baby cow. There was a red tractor and it pulled a little train. Mommy was too big to ride in it, so I went all by myself and I had some alone time, just me and nobody else. I'm a big kid, you know."

Julie startled. She'd known Bay enjoyed the train, but hadn't realized her need for some independence. That was the trouble with being the youngest of the family; either Bay got lumped into the knot of sisters or babied overmuch. As for the oldest of the family…Maybe the stress of being a senior in high school was too much for Lauren. She'd suggest some girl-time on Friday night. Amazing, what a sappy movie and some new nail polish could do for one's spirits.

"You *are* a big girl, that's right." Savannah smiled at Bay. "I have a bunch of homework to do. How about if you sit here by me and we can work on our papers together? You can practice your letters. That way, when you start school, you'll be ready."

"Thanks, Vannie!" Bay set out a sheet of paper, her pencil poised. "Tell me how to spell orange."

Lauren came in, dropping her backpack on the floor, her face a storm cloud. The door slammed behind her. "Bay, write S.T.U.P.—"

"Lauren Rae!" Julie scolded. "How will she learn words are important if we don't teach her right? Savannah, help Bay spell orange." She trailed Lauren up the stairs to her room. "Lauren, what's gotten into you? Are you in some trouble? A bad grade?"

"Worse than that." Lauren's face crumpled. She slammed the door shut and threw herself on the bed, sobbing, her face buried in the pillow. "Infinitesimally, incredibly, infinitely worse than that. It's too horrible to talk about. Don't even ask."

Julie's mind raced. What could be worse for her studious daughter than a bad grade? Oh, no, surely not…she wasn't pregnant, was she? Not with such a bright future ahead of her! Julie's neck tightened. Why, if Beck had—

Lauren sat up and flung her arms out wide, tears flowing. "Mother, what am I going to do? I didn't mean to—"

"Listen, Lauren, it'll be okay. You're young, but you're healthy." Julie pulled Lauren into an embrace, ignoring the mascara tears staining her shirt. "It's not going to be easy with a baby in the house, but we'll figure this out. Together. We'll get through this, I promise."

Chapter Thirty-Four

"A…a what? A baby?" Lauren recoiled with a jolt, her face white. "Mother, what are you talking about? Are you *pregnant?* How could you let that happen? Who is he? Ewww."

"Me?" Julie stared at her daughter. "I'm not even seeing anyone. Of course, I'm not pregnant. *You* are. And it'll be—"

"Mother! *I'm* not pregnant!" Lauren protested, her cheeks flaming. "Unless the laws of biology changed overnight, there's no way I could be. Not that it's any of your business. Good grief, with a houseful of sisters, why on earth would you think I'd want to have a baby? I'm not even out of high school yet!"

They stared at each other. At last Julie ventured, "If you're not going to have a baby, what are you so upset about?"

"Well, I gotta say, after you scared me like that, it doesn't seem nearly as important as it did an hour ago." Lauren flounced on her bed, eyes downcast. "Mr Hendricks called me in after art class. He'd received a letter from Smithson University."

"That exclusive private school in Oregon? Lauren, we talked about this." Julie reached her hand to touch Lauren's. "With all five of you girls to get through college, there's just no way we can afford an elite college. I'm sorry, honey, but the state university has some good programs, too."

"That's just it. I'm fine going to U of M. They have a good pre-med department. I applied there, but the school insisted I apply at three universities. Just for fun, I applied at Smithson, too." She wiped her nose as tears began again. "And they want me. I've been accepted."

"Oh, sweetie, that's wonderful!" Julie beamed, then her face fell. "But there's just no way we can afford that tuition. What was it, $45,000 a year? With Savannah right behind you...I'm sorry."

"I know, Mother, I get that. The thing is..." Lauren wailed, "It's a full ride scholarship, housing, fees, tuition, all of it! Even a $1200 per month stipend. What am I going to do?" Lauren flung herself flat on the bed, sobbing into her pillow.

"Okay, okay, pull yourself together." Julie awkwardly patted her back. "Let me get this straight. A terrific university with a world-renowned pre-med program likes you, they're willing to pay for you to go there, and you're bawling. Help me understand."

Lauren mumbled something.

In the distance, the doorbell rang. Julie heard the stampede of feet rushing to answer the door. "Sit up. I can't understand you."

"I said, I love Beck and I'm not leaving him behind. I can't go to Oregon without him." Lauren pulled the pillow away from her face. "*Oregon?* What am I, some old pioneer? But, Mother, a scholarship to a university that good is a miracle. I can't believe they want me."

A timid tap came at the bedroom door. "Lauren, can I come in? Savannah said you were up here."

Julie jumped up, nearly colliding with Lauren who raced for the bathroom. "Beck? Did she also tell you our house rule of no boys in the bedroom?"

"Mother, no! Tell him I can't see him!" Lauren hissed from the doorway.

"Sorry, Ms Julie, but I want to talk to Lauren. You can stay, of course."

"Thank you for that." Julie shook her head and opened the door, ignoring a growl from the bathroom. Some days were more so than others. Beck's eyes looked unnaturally bright. The girls had said he'd missed school. A fever, perhaps? "Tell you what, Beck. Lauren needs a minute to …uh…regroup… so how about you and I go downstairs until she's ready?" Over her shoulder, Julie flung at the bathroom door, "I'm *sure* she'll hurry."

Usually talkative, Beck sat at the kitchen table, silent, a distant expression in his eyes. The girls surrounded him, their eyes wary. What had he done to their sister?

Fifteen minutes later, Julie snapped. "Look, Beck, you can't keep drumming on the table like that. Eat another cookie and I'll go see what's keeping Lauren."

Julie sighed as she hiked up the long curving staircase. What a crazy day. On the one hand, she knew Lauren deserved the scholarship. She'd worked hard for those grades, even added extra online classes. On the other hand, Oregon was over two thousand miles away. On the other hand, it was an honor, certainly not something she could turn down lightly, and what a gift to have a full scholarship! On the other hand, the state university had a good program, too. On the other hand, if she turned down the scholarship to Smithson, Lauren might regret it the rest of her life. On the other hand, love was love and it looked to Julie that her daughter and Beck were in it deep. She couldn't imagine leaving Dan to go away at this stage of their relationship long ago. On the other hand, a girl had to think of her future, and Lauren needed to finish her education. On the other hand, did it matter so much *where* she studied? On the other hand...

A few more "other hands" and I can build a fine octopus. Where's Dan when I need him?

She pushed open Lauren's door after tapping. "Goodness, what are you thinking? You can't be in bed in your pajamas this time of day. You know Beck is waiting downstairs."

"I'm not coming down," Lauren pouted. "This day is too much for me. I'm declaring a self-care day. Me and my organic chemistry assignment, that's all I'm doing today. If I feel ambitious later on, I might have a bubble bath."

"Oh, no, you don't, Daughter." Julie tugged at the comforter. "You should be excited. A scholarship! Dad would be so proud of you."

"Mother, try to see my point of view, will you?" Lauren sniffed. "Yeah, I get good grades, but I can't handle this. I'm not an adult. I'm just a kid and I don't know what to do."

Julie surveyed Lauren's tear-streaked face and the pile of wadded tissues on the nightstand. When was the last time Lauren put her hair in pigtails? "Okay, I'll tell Beck to go away. Take a break, you've earned it." She headed toward the door in time to hear feet thundering up the staircase.

"Mommy said no boys in the bedrooms," Holly yelled. "You're not supposed to be up here!"

Beck pushed Lauren's door open. She yelped and ducked her head under the blanket.

"Sorry, Lauren. I know I'm invading your space and I'm sorry, but I really need to tell you something." Beck stood awkwardly in the doorway, his eyes on the pink carpet. "Please?"

"Go away!" Lauren wailed.

"That's the thing, that's what I'm trying to say. I *am* going away. Dad says I have no choice." In a sea of girls, Beck looked downright pitiful. "Lauren, please talk to me."

"Hear him out." A wave of pity washed over Julie. "Lauren, come out of that blanket right now."

Lauren slowly lowered the comforter. "You're… leaving me? I thought you loved me. Beck, how could you?" She jumped to her feet, pigtails flying. "Get out then! I never want to see you again, do you hear me?" She burst into tears, dove under her comforter, and wailed, "All of you, just leave me alone!"

Beck fled under a hail of thrown pillows. Larkin and Holly followed him down the stairs, shouting. "You go away! You made our sister cry!"

"Savannah, get the door, will you? Of all times for someone to drop by," Julie barked, tossing a fresh box of tissues on the bed. "Lauren, you go ahead and cry, then we'll sort this all out."

"Mom, it's Mr Hendricks," Larkin called. "He wants to talk to you and Lauren. He says it's important."

Chapter Thirty-Five

"Tell Mr Hendricks we'll be down soon," Julie called down the stairs. "*Both* of us," she said to the lump under Lauren's comforter. She sat on the bed, waiting until her daughter emerged, dragging her feet on her way to the bathroom.

A couple of minutes later, Lauren reappeared in jeans and sweater, her pigtails gone, red-eyed but dry-faced.

"Come on." Julie took her hand. "You look like you're going to meet your doom. You won a full scholarship—you should be elated."

"Elation is for happy people, not girls whose one-and-only broke up with them."

"Honey, we'll talk about that later. One thing at a time." Julie draped her arm around Lauren's sagging shoulders. "Don't start crying again; you'll smear your mascara."

A giggle escaped Lauren's lips, followed by a massive sniff. "Even if I do, it won't look as bad as that photo in the family album, the one where you looked like a wet raccoon with a cheesy smile."

"Hey, I'll have you know that mascara was all the rage back in the day." Julie poked her playfully. "It came in cakes with a little brush, and we had to use a drop of water to apply it. Heaven help us if it rained. Dan and I were dating, on a picnic that day. Not my fault the clouds opened up." She smiled. "Your dad said I was beautiful and snapped my picture, half under the picnic blanket. I wondered then about his eyesight. Did you see my dripping hair?"

"He really loved you, didn't he? I remember him saying you were the best thing in his whole life." Lauren laid her head on Julie's shoulder with a heavy sigh.

"It'll be that way for you one day, too, I promise. If you and Beck are meant for each other, things will work out. If not, that means God has another plan in store for you. Have a little faith. Come on, let's not keep the superintendent waiting."

From the bottom step, Julie surveyed the silent front room. Mr Hendricks sat on the divan, fingering his hat, clearly ill at ease under the gaze of the girls across the room on the settee. Beck shifted from one foot to the other by the side table, looking like he'd rather be just about anywhere else. Bay threw another block at his foot.

"Hello, Mr Hendricks." Julie extended her hand. "Sorry for the delay."

"Good to see you, Julie. I hope this is not a bad time for your family. I come bearing good news and congratulations, but I must say, I've been in more cheerful funeral homes." He glanced at Beck's stormy face. "I do hope all is well."

"Just some miscommunication." Julie took a seat, pulling Lauren down beside her. "Savannah, please bring in some of those cookies, will you?"

Savannah shot a glare at Beck that would have melted a meeker man as she passed.

"I'm sorry," he choked. "Mr Hendricks told me to stay."

Lauren folded her arms, refusing to make eye contact with him.

"Now, Mr Hendricks, what can we help you with?" Julie smiled. *And make it quick, I have a broken heart to patch.*

"I would have assumed our Lauren here would have told you her good news," he began. "We here in Grant County pride ourselves on our excellent students and partial scholarships are frequently attained by our graduating seniors. Lauren, however, has been awarded one of only two full scholarships in the history of Grant County school district. Thank you, Savannah. Oatmeal raisin?" He took a bite of the cookie. "A full scholarship is a wonderful honor for our school. And how fortuitous that they are both in the same school year."

"I am very proud of Lauren." Julie glanced at Lauren's downcast face and mentally drummed her fingers. *Get to the point, will you?* "And a full scholarship *is* a huge blessing."

"It is, indeed. I was hoping the two families might be willing to be honored in a celebration marking this great accomplishment. It would serve to encourage our younger students as well. Will the evening of the eighteenth work for your family?"

"I believe so." Julie shot a glance at Lauren. "Just tell me what you need us to do."

"Why, nothing. I had in mind a dinner for the community, a few short speeches, perhaps some dancing."

At a snort from Savannah, his face reddened. "*Short*, I said."

"That sounds lovely. Thank you." Julie asked, "Now, you said there are two students. May I ask who the other is?"

The superintendent straightened his jacket, glancing at his shoes. "I…that is…I assumed, under the circumstances—"

Julie stared at him. Why the secrecy? The girls looked from one adult to the other, their heads moving like tennis balls across a net.

After a long pause, Beck cleared his throat. "Me. It's me. That's why I came here. I wanted to tell—"

"You? Why didn't you say something?" Lauren flew at him like a wet cat. "Now you'll go away to college somewhere across the country and I'll never see you again. How could you do this to me?"

Julie grabbed her arm and sat her firmly on the side chair. "Honey, it'll all work out—"

Mr Hendricks rose to Beck's defense. "Young man, I suggest you explain yourself, and make it fast." His deep voice brooked no argument.

"I love you, Lauren." Beck held out his arms. "I want to be with you the rest of my life."

"No way, I'm not getting into any long-distance relationship." Lauren fought tears and failed.

She wailed, "You just go to your old university without me!"

"I'm trying to tell you. Lauren, I don't want to be without you. I got into Smithson, too, full ride. We can go together, study together, maybe even share some classes."

"Smithson?" Lauren stared, not comprehending. "You did? You really did? We can go together?"

Julie looked from her daughters, one sobbing on her boyfriend's chest, the others in an open-mouthed row on the sofa, to the school superintendent, who mopped his brow, clearly baffled. Bay lobbed another block at Beck's leg.

"Do you have any children of your own, Mr Hendricks?"

Chapter Thirty-Six
A year later

Dan, it's summer again, and I can't believe how much has happened in the last year. Can you believe we're going to be—

"Ms Julie, are you in the kitchen?" Beck called from the back step.

"Yes, come on in." Julie pulled the last pan of tarts from the oven. "Lauren's not home; she took the girls to the park. I thought you'd be with them. Have an apple tart while they're still warm."

"I'm on my way there now." He twisted his keyring in his hand. "Ms Julie, I need to ask a favor."

"Sure, Beck, what do you need?" She pulled out a chair. "Everything okay? You look agitated."

"I…I guess I am, a little, Ms Julie—"

"Beck, how many times have I told you? You're old enough to call me just Julie."

He sat, twining his long legs around the chair legs. Bit a tart, chewed it slowly, his eyes on the table. "Can I call you Mom instead?"

"What? I …guess so. But why?"

"Well, I love Lauren and I want to marry her—"

"No surprise. Everybody knows you're meant for each other. Soon as you two get your education."

"I mean sooner than that," Beck's voice sped up. "Real soon, if it's okay with you, before fall semester starts. We don't want to wait until we graduate. With our scholarships and stipends, we can make ends meet and set quite a bit aside, too. It makes sense to be together. You said it yourself, we're meant to be." He smiled that slow smile. "Lauren doesn't know I've got it all calculated out. I need your help figuring out how to propose to her. You know she loves a surprise. If you're okay with us getting married, I mean."

"Wow, this came on fast." Julie blinked and considered. On the one hand, Lauren is young, not yet twenty years old. On the other hand, she has a good head on her shoulders; they both do. On the other hand, would marriage distract her from her education? Dan and I agreed our kids would be college-educated long before any of them were born. On the other hand, Lauren's too smart to waste a full scholarship and she loves her classes. On the other hand, what if babies came along? On the other hand, Beck clearly adores Lauren, and she him. What's the point of getting in their way? On the other hand, that's not much time to plan a wedding.

A few other hands…again with the octopus.

"I approve," Julie wagged a finger and smiled. "So long as you make sure she graduates. Both of you."

"I sure will; Lauren is scorching smart."

Julie hugged Beck. "Well, then, how are you going to propose to her?"

"I was thinking, Mom…"

Dan, we're going to be in-laws! I knew Lauren and Beck were in love—anybody could tell that—but I admit I'm surprised the wedding is coming on this fast. Who else pulls off a wedding on only three months? Lauren, that's who. Beck is a good young man.

You'd like Beck. He reminds me a lot of you, with that easy grin and the way he jumps right into any project. He's got some skills, too, from working with his dad. Never met a boy who gets excited studying statistics, but he also loves to hike and camp and do all the things Lauren does. Well, except shopping; I can't say I blame him there. The girls love him— they treat him like a big brother. I know you'd like him. Wait, Dan, are you the one who sent him to Lauren? Please, darling, keep watching over our family and pull heavenly strings if you need to. How I miss you.

Beck planned a nice proposal for Lauren. He said he and his dad were going up to Perfume Lake on Saturday and invited our family along, casual as could be. He and the girls packed a picnic. After everybody played for a while, Beck called out and said his foot was caught on something. He was about hip deep in the lake. The girls swam over and Savannah pulled it up, an old blue jar with a lid and something inside. Beck carried it to shore and kept a straight face, too.

Everybody went to see what was inside it. Bay was pretty sure it was a frog family's house.

Beck had Lauren unscrew the lid. She pulled out one of those little wooden treasure boxes, the kind you get at the craft stores. Inside was a note that read A Love Gained Is Nevermore Lost. The girls puzzled over it, wondering how long it'd been down in the water. Larking decided it must be a secret code of some kind. Beck said he'd worked up an appetite. That boy has a poker face, let me tell you.

After lunch, he passed out the little dessert cups they'd made in mini mason jars. We all ate, talking, laughing, and them Lauren got a funny look on her face. She pulled a little plastic ring out of her mouth, totally baffled. By then, Beck was on one knee holding out a real ring in a velvet box. You should have heard the girls' squeals when she said "Yes." Maybe you did hear them. How far is heaven?

And now tomorrow is their wedding day. Julie patted one recalcitrant curl, then settled into her window seat. *Lauren's so happy, she absolutely glows like the ladies in those sappy romance books Margaret reads. Is there no other way for a writer to describe a happy face without glowing about it?* She stared out the window. *There are so many stars tonight. Are you one of them, looking down on us, Dan?*

Chapter Thirty-Seven

"Mother, can you keep my bouquet safe? Bay keeps trying to pull the ribbons out of it and I can't chase after her in this dress." Lauren clipped her white feather headpiece in her hair and smoothed her hair. "Is that the right angle, do you think? I probably should have gone with the tea-length dress, but I wanted Beck to see me in a real wedding gown, you know?"

"Just a little more to the front, I think." Julie sighed. "I'll get Connor to ride herd on Bay. She's so excited about your wedding, he'll have to catch her first. You are stunning, daughter. I'm so glad you found Beck. It's easier to go through life with someone to hold hands with."

"I really love him." Lauren blotted her lipstick and dabbed at a sudden tear. "I wish Daddy was here today. I miss him so much."

"I do, too, honey. You have so many people who love you and are coming to support you and Beck, but I miss him, too. Don't cry or your nose will be red in the pictures." Julie glanced at the open bedroom door. "Connor? Is everything all right?"

"Lauren, you are a vision of all that's lovely." Dan's father gave a low whistle. "I don't think there has ever been a more beautiful bride. Except maybe you, Julie. It's close, if you're competing." He stepped in. "My favorite oldest granddaughter is marrying a fine young man in less than an hour and all is right with the world. I just wanted to see if you needed anything from me." He chuckled. "And I had to get away from that woman downstairs, the one setting up the punchbowls. Badgering me like a mosquito on a damp summer night."

"Elsie? What did she say?"

"She says since Dan is gone, it's my duty to walk our Lauren down the aisle and give her away. My bounden duty, that's how she put it."

"I—" Lauren turned.

"I know, I told her." He held up his hand. "I told her nobody can give you away. You're a treasure, but not a commodity to be handed over like a plate of cookies. You own your own heart, Lauren."

"But I don't want to hurt your feelings, Grandpa." Lauren took his hand. "I love you, you know. If you want—"

"No, Ma'am! This is your day and I want you to have it just as your heart desires. Besides, I'll have me a catbird seat if I sit beside your mama and not have to get in anybody's way."

Julie jumped at the alarm on Lauren's phone. "Good grief, daughter, it's your wedding day! It's not as though you'll be late to class."

"I've seen enough weddings where the bride makes everybody wait. Not me—I can't wait to be Beck's wife." She set the phone on the dresser. "There, that's my last alarm of the day. I'm meeting him by the gate so we can pray together before our wedding. And so he can see my dress. I do look nice, don't I?" She kissed Julie and Connor. "Love you both, and Mother, please protect my bouquet."

After Lauren slipped down the back staircase, Julie pulled her father-in-law to the bow window overlooking the side yard. Unseen by guests gathering in the back garden, Lauren darted across the lawn, holding her skirt above the new-mown grass. She must have called to Beck; as she approached, he turned to her. She ran into his embrace, and there they stood in the dappled light, emanating a joy even the angels admired.

"They're so in love, it makes my heart dance." Julie caught a movement in the hedge by the corner of the house. "Oh, good, the photographer spotted them, but I don't think Lauren or Beck noticed her. Those pictures will be wonderful. Lauren prefers candid shots."

"Even if they see her, I don't think they care a whit. Their minds are on each other, the way it looks to me." Connor smiled. "I heard Larkin and Holly talking downstairs. They were sure Lauren's young man would cry when he saw her in her wedding dress." He chuckled. "Smart man. Look, he's wiping his eyes, but he'll get that out of his system before the music starts."

"Come on, we'd better get down there before Bay and Holly dismantle the wedding cake." Julie linked arms with him. "And I'll protect you from Elsie, too."

Dan, the wedding was gorgeous. I'm glad Lauren decided to have it here at Glyth House. Julie kicked off her heels six hours later. *My feet are killing me from all that dancing. The back garden's flowers perfumed the air, and I swear, even the bees were smiling. Lauren was a beautiful bride. The way Beck looks at her is so sweet. Reminds me of you when we were young, as if he's not even aware the rest of the world exists when Lauren's around. They're off to Gull Lake Resort for a quick honeymoon. With their next semester starting in a couple of weeks, they barely have time for that, what with moving their stuff and settling in. They're so happy.*

I hope I taught Lauren all she needs to know. I still have the other girls to finish raising and I'm sure Lauren will be calling on me as she and Beck begin their life together. I'm a mother-in-law, Dan! The day was lovely, but there was a hole in the festivities, a hole that was your place. She frowned at her image in the mirror and yanked out a grey hair.

Why am I growing old without you?

Chapter Thirty-Eight
a year and a half later

"Mom, I had an idea."

Julie swallowed a sigh. Of all times—! "Savannah, I hope it doesn't require my help. I'm still tired from that bout of flu." Julie looked up from painting the doorframe. "And with trying to get this room ready for when Julie and Beck come to visit, I'm not up to tackling another big project."

"It's not a huge project, and it'll be fun. You're always saying we need to be involved in the community. And I think Grandpa's a little bored living here. With Grandma getting more and more confused, all he does is take care of her and help her tend the flowers in the conservatory."

"Okay, then, what's on your mind?"

"Tansy's conservatory is so pretty with all that glass, like an elegant Victorian greenhouse. It's even better at night, with the soft lighting and so many stars in the sky. Grandpa repaired all the little leaks. Grandma loves tending the flowers in there. He says it helps her stay calm." Savannah said, "You know how he loves to talk to people and tell stories to everybody. You should have seen him yesterday when we stopped at the diner in town. He said we were just going in for a slice of pie, but we were there over an hour. No matter where he goes, he draws a crowd around him."

"He sure does love to tell stories, that's true. And they're interesting ones, most of the time." Julie shuddered. "I do wish he'd stop telling the one my mother told him about me in Japan when I was four and I got into the cooking oil and made the kitchen floor into a skating rink."

"The fact that you were naked makes it a better story," Savannah chuckled.

"I didn't want to ruin my outfit," Julie defended herself. "And really, do people need to think about me like that?"

"It's still funny. Anyway, I was thinking about Grandpa's stories about the orphanage and his mission trips. Seems people around here don't travel much, and I know they love hearing about his adventures. You missed a spot." Savannah dabbed a paint brush on the window frame. "What would you think about holding a story night, where people could come and listen to him?"

"Oh, I can just see that! I remember Tansy telling me about gatherings a lot like that. I think she called them salons. There'd be some kind of entertainment, a speaker or pianist or cellist or something, and people would pay a quarter for the evening. Then the money would go to some good cause. Is that what you have in mind?"

"I doubt a quarter would even cover the cost of the refreshments, but, yes. I'm thinking we could serve dessert and I could help Grandpa convert his photos into a slide show."

"It's a fine idea. How many are you thinking about inviting?"

"If we brought down those folding wooden chairs from the attic, I think we could seat as many as sixty." Savannah considered. "Maybe it'd make more sense to hold it in the ballroom upstairs, but the conservatory is so much nicer. What do you think?"

"I vote for the conservatory. The third-floor ballroom is too big for this kind of event, and Grandpa would hate using a microphone. He's likely to draw a crowd of elderly people, and those stairs get longer every time. Besides, you're right, the conservatory is beautiful."

Julie stood and stretched. "I remember Tansy had a tea service for a lot of people. I could help you hunt it down; it must be stored somewhere."

"Thanks, Mom. I think Grandpa will love it. He and Grandma can show off their flowers at the same time, if she's up to it."

"Go ahead, plan it out, but remember your sister will be here next week. And Beck, too."

"Beck hasn't heard most of Grandpa's stories. We'll have it a week from Saturday. I'd better get on this."

"Fine, but don't rope Lauren into helping. She's almost eight months along, and that's not a good stage for climbing on chairs or baking dozens of tarts. They're coming here to rest after their final exams, remember."

"I know. She said it's their last trip before the baby arrives. Do you think the baby will have red hair like Dad?"

Chapter Thirty-Nine

"Bay, quit running back and forth to the window. You're making me dizzy." Julie smiled at her youngest. "Their flight landed an hour ago. They'll be here soon, but you're not making the time pass any faster. Go read or something."

"Look, Mommy, I made a book for Lauren." Bay held a rumpled construction paper packet, stapled on the left side. "See, I drew a picture of the baby on the front."

"Show me." Julie set the broom aside. "Is that a baby? It looks like..."

Holly glanced at the booklet and grimaced. "It looks like a fish."

"It's not a fish!" Bay protested. "It's a baby whale."

"What?" Larkin ruffled her hair. "Lauren's not having a whale, silly goose."

"She told Mommy on the phone she's as big as a whale. We haven't seen it yet, have we? I think she'll have a baby whale." Bay let out a yelp. "I heard a car door."

Bay ran to the front window. "Lauren and Beck are here! Mommy, you said she was having a baby, but I guess they left it home. I don't see any baby." She flung open the door and ran down the steps. "Lauren, you got fat. Beck, pick me up, pick me up!"

"You little scamp, I'm not fat!" Lauren smiled and rubbed her back. "And that's not self-esteem food."

"You look lovely," Connor said. "Just you wait until your grandmother sees you. She'll say you're expecting a little stranger."

"A stranger, Grandpa?" Holly giggled. "I bet it'll look just like Lauren, and that's pretty strange, all right."

Lauren swatted her with a grin. "Too bad I can't chase you, Holly, for saying that!"

Beck slipped his arm around Lauren. "Our baby is going to be beautiful, just like Lauren."

"Oh, I'm so glad you made it!" Julie hugged Lauren and smiled at Beck. "You must be tired. Come on in. I have sandwiches."

"Good, I'm hungry. All I do these days is eat, seems to me." Lauren settled into a chair. "Feels good to be out of the car."

"Our first great-grandchild is going to be pretty special. Grandma's going to love it so much." Grandpa took his seat at the table. "Do you know if it's a girl or boy?"

"I sure *hope* it's a girl or a boy. If it's a puppy, I'm going to be very disappointed." Lauren laughed. "We're not telling until the baby's born safely. A lot can go wrong and we're not jinxing it."

As they settled in at the kitchen table, Bay said, "I like puppies. Mommy, if Lauren doesn't want her puppy, can I have it?"

"That's enough, you guys, let me catch my breath." Lauren sighed. "Not an easy task these days, let me tell you. Where's Savannah and Larkin?"

"She and Larkin went shopping and took Grandma along to help pick out tablecloths." Julie set a platter of sub sandwiches on the table. "Did she tell you about the event on Saturday?"

"Yes, a salon, she called it. If Grandpa's telling stories, I can't wait. Pass the chips, please."

As they ate, Beck bragged, "Can you believe Lauren took highest honors in every one of her classes? I'm really proud of her."

"Your grades were really high, too," Lauren blushed. "Best study-buddy ever."

"True, but I didn't start the year with morning sickness. I still think taking a full load of credits was too much, yet you did it."

"Ewww, Mommy, he's kissing her!"

"It's okay, Bay. They're married." Holly elbowed her. "Oh, Savannah and Larkin are back, and Grandma."

Savannah hurried in, her arms full of shopping bags. "Hey, you guys! Glad to see you. You're just in time to help me."

Marsha leaned on Larkin's arm as she climbed the steps into the kitchen, her pace slow. "Oh, we have company? Hello, dear, my name is Marsha."

Lauren turned stricken eyes to Julie. She mouthed, "She doesn't know us?"

"Now, Marsha, it's Lauren and Beck." Julie said, "Your granddaughter. You remember their wedding, and now they've come from college for a visit."

Marsha closed her eyes, her brow furrowed in concentration. She shrugged. "Well, it's lovely to meet you. Are you expecting a little stranger, dear?"

"Yes, Grandma, the baby is due in five weeks. Beck and I wanted to come see you all while I can still travel."

"That's nice, dear." Marsha wandered out of the kitchen.

"Mother! You didn't tell me she was that bad off." Lauren watched her go. "She didn't even know us."

"The doctors say her dementia is increasing, but she's healthy."

"Now, you're not to worry about her." Connor spooned potato salad onto his plate. "She has her good times and bad. Shopping probably took all of her energy. After a little rest, she'll be fine. I'll make sure she eats something when she wakes up."

"Oh, Grandpa, I'm sorry I'm not here to help." Lauren wiped a tear.

"Now, don't go getting sad on me. Moving here to Glyth House has been a blessing and your mother and sisters have been good to us. The doctors say the worst thing for Marsha would be to just sit around in a chair, getting old. Your sisters keep her mind active, you can be sure of that. I know she's going to enjoy your sister's get-together tomorrow night."

"Savannah, tell us about it. Why did you call it a salon?" Lauren set her glass on the table. "That sounds so old-fashioned."

"It's supposed to. We're having gingerbread with cream and little mints, plus orange herbal tea served in Tansy's teacups. Grandpa's going to tell about their mission trip in Ecuador. Already, sixty-four people signed up to attend, and more will probably show up at the door."

"Well, I think it sounds wonderful. Maybe seeing the old pictures will be good for Grandma." Lauren smiled. "One of the advantages of being married to a tall man is that I can volunteer his help, right, Beck? Personally, I'm just going to watch. My back has been killing me. I think this baby enjoys kicking my spine."

"At your service," Beck grinned. "Since Savannah called and asked me to be on chair-set-up duty, I thought of a way to get those old wooden chairs down from the third floor. They fold, right? Any reason we can't tie a few together and lower them on a rope through the window?"

"See there, everybody? I told you he'll be a fine engineer." Lauren winked at him. "May I have more lemonade, please?"

Chapter Forty

Julie woke to thumps against the side of the house. "It's barely dawn! What are they doing?" She rolled over and groaned. "The chairs? Was Beck serious about using a rope?" She stumbled to the window and stuck her head out. "Be careful out there!"

"Good morning, Mom. Hope we didn't wake you." Savannah guided a belay line from the ground as Beck sent four folding chairs to the grass beside her. Larkin quickly untied the rope and he pulled it back up.

"Have you guys slept at all?" Julie rubbed her eyes. "Do I smell gingerbread?"

"Lauren was up about four o'clock," Beck called down. "Said she couldn't sleep. I think her back is hurting from the plane ride yesterday."

"She makes the best gingerbread." Savannah swung the line wide, barely missing Larkin.

"What are you thinking? You'll need at least six pans of it. Did you forget she's pregnant?"

"How could anybody forget that? Have you *seen* her? She looks like she swallowed a beachball, the big, expensive kind. And anyway, Larkin is helping her, and we'll go in as soon as we get all the chairs down. Good idea of Beck's, don't you think?"

The day passed quickly, with all hands on deck. Except Marsha; Connor insisted she nap so she could enjoy the evening.

"Child, are you in pain?" Connor found Lauren in the kitchen mid-afternoon, bent over with her head on the counter.

"No, Grandpa, I'm okay." Lauren stood and forced a smile. "I'm trying to stretch. It feels like someone committed macramé in the small of my back. Guess I'm not designed for being so lopsided."

"I think you're beautiful, and you're going to be a first-class mother. How about I get you a heating pad and you can go rest a bit?"

"There's still so much to do…" she protested, then thought better of it. "You're right, the girls can finish without me."

"I know where your mother keeps the heating pad. I'll bring it to you."

By the time Connor brought the electric heating pad to the front room, Lauren was already asleep on the lounge chair. He gently covered her with a nearby quilt, smoothed a crease from her forehead, and headed toward the conservatory to help the others finish setting up.

"What do you think, Grandpa?" Savannah called from her perch on a step ladder. "One more string of lights, then all we have to do is set out food and make the orange tea."

"It looks terrific. I'd better polish my stories to make them worthy of such an event."

"I'm sure whatever you say will be well received." Julie hurried past him with a stack of linen napkins. "You're a good sport, you know."

"Nonsense. I do have the gift of gab, after all, and I enjoy helping my granddaughters in any project." Connor reconsidered. "On second thought, I did tell Bay last week I wouldn't help her make a paper airplane big enough to ride in. She planned to sail it off the barn roof."

"Thanks for that! That child's creativity knows no bounds." Julie paused and smiled. "It's so good having you and Marsha here with us."

Connor's face reddened. "Ah, you all are the blessing for us. Who else would take in a couple of old, decrepit in-laws when they don't have to?"

"It's been good for us all. You're a good influence on my girls, and I know they appreciate having you here to help them plan new and different forms of mischief." Julie sobered. "I hope tonight won't be too much for Marsha."

"I think she'll love it. Being around people is good for her, the doctors say. I hope nobody minds her forgetting their names." Connor blinked twice and headed toward the kitchen, calling, "Larkin, snitch me a piece of that gingerbread, will you?"

Chapter Forty-One

A couple of hours later, Julie leaned against a post in the back of the conservatory, awed. A goodly crowd sat mesmerized as Connor "waxed eloquent," as he said, laughing in all the right places. Savannah, her face glowing, sat with her boyfriend, hands clasped. It was only a matter of time, Julie sighed. A movement caught her eye. Lauren bent slightly forward and drew a deep breath. Beck leaned in to rub her lower back. The last stage of pregnancy wasn't for wimps. Near the left side, Larkin sat with Marsha and Holly. The elderly woman smiled, entranced by her beloved's familiar stories.

Connor wrapped up his story with, "And that's the truth, more or less" and took a deep bow to warm applause.

Savannah stood. "Grandpa, you were wonderful! Thanks, everybody, for coming. Join us now for light refreshments."

People stood, chatting, milling under the lights strings. Several commented on Tansy's China, recognizing it from earlier days.

"Just like old times, isn't it? Dear Tansy, if she could see the life in Glyth House now!"

"My, this gingerbread is delicious."

"Isn't the conservatory beautiful. Restored to its former glory, I say."

"Savannah, dear, when is the next event? You can be sure we'll be in attendance."

"Where did the donations jar end up? I enjoyed this so much, I need to put more money in it."

Larkin and Savannah served gingerbread and smiles while Julie poured cups of orange tea and fielded compliments.

"No, I had nothing to do with it, they planned it all themselves."

"Yes, Connor is a character, all right."

"Thank you for coming tonight."

Connor stood with his arm around Marsha, protecting her from the crowd. Julie knew he was likely whispering the names of friends and neighbors in her ear, so she'd feel more comfortable. Terrible thing, to lose a memory. Julie mentally counted her daughters as she reached for another teacup. Bay perched between Josiah and Margaret, deep in her gingerbread. Holly stood by Beck and Lauren, talking up a storm. Something about Lauren stirred in Julie's mind. What could it be?

The bathroom.

All day, Lauren had run to the bathroom every hour or so, it seemed to Julie. Now she hadn't moved since Connor took the microphone, and why were her cheeks so flushed?

"Yes, Emily, I agree, he did fine."

"He sure has had some adventures, hasn't he?"

"More tea, Lulu?"

"Thanks for coming."

"Thanks, I'll tell him."

Beck stood and made eye contact with Julie across the conservatory. Julie smiled back, noting a crease on his forehead. He must be concerned about Lauren getting overtired. It'd probably be best for her and Marsha to both get to bed as soon as the guests left. Was there no way to politely encourage people to take their coats and head into the night?

"Mom?" Beck slipped behind the table and murmured in Julie's ear. "Lauren says she needs you. She won't tell me what's wrong. Let me take over, okay?"

Without a word, Julie handed Back a teacup and made her way across the conservatory. Several people stopped her to comment. "Yes, the girls did this all themselves. Thank you, I'll tell them you said so. Good evening."

Finally, Julie sank into the chair beside Lauren. "Are you okay? Beck said—"

"Mother, do you remember a couple of years ago, the day I got the scholarship and I was so upset, and you thought I was pregnant?"

"Of course. I still feel bad for questioning your morals. Even in the heat of a tear storm, I should have known better. Why are you bringing that up now?" Julie took her daughter's hand. "Are you okay? Your face reminds me of a Raggedy Ann doll, with two red circles. Beck said—"

Lauren wiped her forehead. "The thing is, I'm good and pregnant now."

"Yes, anyone can see that." *What on earth? It wasn't overly warm in the conservatory; now that people were taking their leave, the door let in a chilly draft. Was Lauren running a fever?* "Honey, are you feeling alright? Do you need to go rest? Here, let me help you up."

"Well, actually…I can't stand up." Lauren closed her eyes. "The thing is…I seem to have wet myself, which hasn't happened since I was three. And it's not stopping." A single tear ran past her nose. "I can't stand up with all these people here. And I need to."

Julie leaned forward. "Honey, do you think your water broke? You're not in labor, are you?"

"Uh, oh. Maybe." Lauren's mouth gaped open and closed like a goldfish. "I have a dull ache in my back that comes and goes, but I thought it was muscle spasms. The baby's not due for another five weeks. Mother, what am I going to do?"

Chapter Forty-Two

"You're going to have a baby, that's what you're going to do. And you're going to be okay." Julie hugged her. "Stay put for a minute."

"I told you, I can't stand up—"

Julie patted her daughter's shoulder and walked to Beck. ""Lauren's alright, but I think you're going to be a father before long. Her water broke. I'll send Larkin to get a towel. You go sit with her."

"The baby? It's too early—" Beck blanched.

"Babies can't read calendars. They come when they come." Julie touched his arm. "It's going to be fine. Go to Lauren."

He nodded and moved swiftly across the room, dodging guests.

Julie walked across the room and whispered to Connor, "Lauren's in labor. The baby's coming."

"Already?" He squeezed Marsha's arm. "What do you need me to do?"

"Just help me figure out how to clear folks out. This was great, but we have to help Lauren."

Connor nodded. "I'll get Savannah on that. It's her evening."

Julie motioned to Larkin, who was standing by Holly. "Larkin, run and bring a bath towel. Lauren's water broke."

"What did she break?" Holly puzzled. "There's no water. Did she spill her tea?"

"No, that means her baby is going to be born soon." Julie whispered in Holly's ear.

Savannah listened to Connor then picked up the microphone. "Everyone, thanks so much for coming tonight. I'm truly sorry to break up the party, but we're having a situation our family needs to attend to. Drive safely, and we'll see you at our next gathering."

As people murmured and moved toward the coat racks, Holly shouted. "We're not having a situation, we're having a baby! I'm going to be an aunt!"

Guests laughed, then picked up their coats and moved toward the open door, calling well wishes.

"Holly has a big mouth." Lauren caught her breath and leaned against Beck. "And I think she's right. This baby is on its way."

Once the coast was clear, Beck helped Lauren to the upstairs bathroom; she'd decided a warm bath in the deep clawfoot tub was what she needed. Julie asked Connor to help the little girls get ready for bed. Josiah sat with Marsha, who dozed in her chair. Margaret came up behind Julie in the kitchen.

"Margaret, good of you to stay." Julie offered her a seat. "I've never been a grandmother before, and I need all the help I can get. As soon as Lauren gets out of the tub and dressed, I'll go with her and Beck to the medical center."

"You'll do just fine, dear. I heard Connor reading a story to the girls. I can help him get the little ones to bed, if you'd like."

"That'd be great. You're a good friend."

"Mom, Beck said Lauren needs you." Savannah skidded into the kitchen. "Come quick!"

Julie ran up the wide staircase, taking the steps two at a time. In the upper hallway, she slowed her breathing. "Lauren, honey, what's going on?"

Beck opened the front bedroom door. "Oh, good, you're here. The contractions are coming pretty close together. What should we do next?"

"Lauren, you're okay." Julie smiled encouragement at her daughter, who was in the rocker, groaning. "Here, let's get your shoes on. They're expecting you at the med center."

"No. I'm not going." Lauren let out a deep breath as the contraction ended.

"Yes, we have to go," Beck said. "The baby's coming."

"I know that, you goose," Lauren snapped. "That's the problem, the baby's coming fast. I can't bear the idea of all those stairs and a car ride into town. No, I'm not going. And you can't make me."

"But, darling, the baby…" Beck took her hand and she batted it away.

"Lauren, be reasonable." Julie soothed, her heart pounding. *Of all times for Lauren's famous stubborn streak to surface.* "Beck is right. Where is your coat?"

As another contraction began, Lauren gasped, "My back hurts so much. Push on my back." Once it eased, she snapped, "I'm not going anywhere. Mother, you always say Glyth House is our home. Generations have been born here and my baby is going to be born in this very room. Instead of arguing with me, can you help me do what I need to do?"

Julie stared at her then sighed. "Beck, we can't reason with her when she gets like this. And the contractions *are* pretty close together. She might not make it to the med center. A home birth is better than one in the car."

Pale, Beck squared his shoulders. "Tell me what to do."

"Just help her find a comfortable position. I'll get what we need. Lauren, you can do this." Julie squeezed her daughter's hand and stepped out into the hallway. On her way down the stairs, she pulled out her cell phone and dialed. "Dr Simms? Are you up for a house call?"

By the time she reached the front room, Julie had a plan and began barking orders. "Lauren's going to have the baby tonight, here at Glyth House. The doctor and a nurse are on their way. Connor, can you keep the girls occupied? They're probably too wound up to sleep. Holly, Bay, you stay with Grandpa and keep out of the way. Marsha's asleep, right? Good. Larkin, tell Margaret we're having a home birth. She'll know what to do, and you help her, okay? Savannah, you're the go-fer; whatever we need, you get it. First thing, that plastic drop cloth from the closet, the new one. And some fresh bed sheets; once they've been through the dryer, they're sterile. Josiah—"

"This isn't my first rodeo. I'll sets some pots of water to boiling and turn on the lights for the doctor." He grinned. "A new baby coming to Glyth House. Imagine that?"

A groan wafted down the stairs, followed by Lauren's cry. "Oh, my gosh, something slipped that time. The baby's coming!"

Julie bolted up the stairs, praying as she ran.

Chapter Forty-Three

"Well, now, you have a fine granddaughter, and your Lauren is a remarkable young woman." Dr Simms slipped his wool coat on a couple of hours later. "I'll check on her later in the morning."

"Thanks, Joseph," Julie said. "I'm glad you were here."

"You didn't need my help; she was already well on her way before we arrived. That little girl was in a hurry. All I did was congratulate her mama." He shook Julie's hand and opened the door. "Call us if anything changes."

Julie sagged on the bottom step, surveying the room. Margaret and Josiah had dozed off on the loveseat, their grey heads together. After insisting they needed to stay up to meet the baby, Bay and Holly had fallen asleep on the sofa across the room, and Connor had draped a quilt over them. Larkin sat by Savannah on the hearth.

"Mom, we did it," Savannah said softly. "It was amazing, wasn't it?"

"They say birth is God's most common miracle." Julie rubbed her back and yawned. "You were a great help, girls. It was a little hectic there for a bit."

"It's just like Lauren to do things her own way." Connor shook his head with a smile.

"But she didn't even wait for the doctor to show up," Larkin complained.

"The baby came fast, that's for sure." Julie yawned again. "We should get some sleep while we can. It's been a very long day. And remember, Lauren said they'll tell us the baby's name when we're all together in the morning."

Julie hugged her daughters and Connor. Once again, she trudged up the front staircase, slower this time.

Just as she passed the front bedroom door, Beck stepped out. "Oh, good, I'm glad you're awake. Lauren was asking for you. Have you ever seen anything more beautiful in your life? " He pushed open the bedroom door. In the glow of the table lamp, Lauren sat in the rocker, her new daughter cradled in her arms.

"Lauren, you look like an angel."

"Oh, Mother, come in. I wanted you to get a chance to properly meet your granddaughter, now that things have calmed down. Do you want to hold her?"

"More than anything." Julie reached for the baby and sat on the footstool. "She's gorgeous, isn't she? And a redhead, like your dad. Look at her little mouth. It's like a pink buttonhole."

"I know. I keep looking at her. I can't believe how perfect she is. Doctor Simms said she's a good weight for being a month early."

"How are you feeling?" Julie smiled as the baby opened her slate blue eyes. ""Hi, darling one. So many people love you already. Your aunts are going to adore you, but Mommy and Daddy will protect you."

"Honestly, I feel like I've been run over by a herd of horses, but it's worth it. She's beautiful, isn't she?" Lauren smiled at Beck. "Beck and I decided if you weren't in bed yet, that you deserve a proper introduction. We knew she was a girl for a couple of months, but if we told anybody, the kids would have badgered us about her name. And our minds were made up." She waved her hand in a flourish. "May I present Tansy Daniella Beckett."

"I love her name!" Julie smiled through sudden tears. "Both Dad and Tansy would be honored. In fact, I'm sure they're smiling on you this very minute." She handed the baby to Beck and hugged Lauren. "Get some sleep, honey. You, too, Beck; you were a big support tonight. The sun will be up soon. I'll keep the girls at bay as long as I can."

"I'll sleep as soon as I feed Tansy." Lauren smiled through a yawn. "I heard Larkin tell Savannah they'd bring me breakfast on a tray. If anyone wants to pamper me, I can take it."

Chapter Forty-Four

Julie washed her face and pulled on her old flannel pajamas, the ones Savannah said make her look like a grandmother. *I am a grandmother.* She knelt to pray, thanking God for Tansy Daniella's safe, albeit sudden, birth. And for Lauren's safe delivery. And for the success of Savannah's salon. And for good friends and having Connor and Marsha at Glyth House. And for Holly, who made everyone laugh, and for a good strong community, and for...

What was that sound?

Julie put her ear against the door that connected her bedroom and the one Lauren and Beck were using, and now baby Tansy Daniella, too. Lauren's clear voice wafted through the door, her soprano light on the air. Julie heard Beck ask sleepily, "What song is that?" and Lauren's reply, "I don't know. Mother used to sing it to us kids when we were little."

Be at peace, my little child, loved you are and safe,

God will protect you now, dear little one, throughout all your days.

Turn to Him in trial and love

and he will hold you in His hand

as He did his son, as He does the dove...

Tears sprang to Julie's eyes. She sagged onto the window seat just as the sun's rays rose over the

horizon. That song. That *song*. She remembered
singing it on the night Lauren was born, that night
when her firstborn refused to sleep, wide eyes taking
in her new world with wonder for hours on end. Dan
snored on the chair in the corner, but Julie was as wide
awake as her new daughter.

A nurse came into her hospital room around
three in the morning and scolded her for not sleeping.
"You must get your rest. You just had a baby."

"I know that, but I can't stop looking at her."
Julie stroked Lauren's downy head. "Have you ever
seen a lovelier baby in all your days?"

The nurse allowed that newborn Lauren was
beautiful, then ordered Julie to get some sleep and
turned off the overhead light on her way out. Julie sat
in bed with her daughter on her lap, softly singing
every folk song she could think of, delighting in the
baby's focused gaze. As she sang that one song, rays
of the brand-new morning sun fell across the bedding.
And the infant's eyes closed.

And now Lauren sang that same song to her
own daughter, more than two decades later.

Julie sat in the window seat. *Dan, if you are
near, watch over our girl, will you? Lauren's a mother
now, I'm a grandmother, and you're not here to see it.*

Chapter Forty-Five
Two years later

Julie sat in a shaft of buttery sunlight in the front room. With the younger girls in school, the house's silence pressed on her.

Dan, I'll always love you, but I seem to be talking to you less and less often. I don't want you to think I forgot about you, but I seem to be standing on my own two feet better than I did at first. I'm putting some new photos in the albums and I realized I'd better catch you up. Look.

You can still keep an eye on us, can't you? This stack is from Savannah's high school graduation last month. She made a scrapbook, with ticket stubs and programs and report cards and all, but I still want some photos in my own album. We keep the old album old Tansy made on the sidebar in the front room. Maybe somebody will care about this one I'm working on. No way of telling, as Margaret would say.

I sure miss her and Josiah. It was so strange, them both passing away the same day, but I guess they didn't want to live without the other. I sure understand that. I'm not sure how the rules work in heaven, but I hope you've had a chance to meet them and catch up. They were so good to our girls. We all miss them, but Bay and Holly most of all. The house next door has new owners, a couple from the city. Nice enough, but he took out the gate first thing and that path we'd worn between the houses is nearly grown over. Margaret would have been so proud of Savannah, graduating with honors and heading off to a horticulture degree, after all those hours they spent talking about medicinal plants and all.

See this photo? Can you believe how beautiful our Savannah is? She was just a little girl when you went away. She's smart and talented and funny. You'd adore her, Dan. And we're all so proud of her, getting a scholarship to MSU. Oh, the writing on top of her mortarboard? It's a verse from a poem she wrote, about being strong when strong is the only choice you have, about living without fear once the worst thing you can imagine happening happed and you're still here. It's not as morbid as it sounds. Upbeat, actually.

I don't have the pictures back from Lauren's and Beck's graduation yet. I'm still amazed Lauren graduated with honors, with her baby boy due next month. Little Tansy was the hit of the party. We've only been back from Oregon a week. It was a little crazy, having all three of them graduate a week apart, and across the country, too. Quite a celebration, let me tell you. The only thing missing was you.

It's been a season of passing, I guess that's one way of looking at it. I'm not sure if you're able to keep up on the news where you are, Dan. With your mother gone, Connor is determined to get a bed and breakfast running. He's been talking about it since the first day he saw Glyth House. It'll be good for him to be busy, and even with just the three younger girls at home, I can use the help.

Holly still talks about seeing Miss Ellie every so often, but it no longer freaks us out. The music box still plays once in a while. I kind of like it; it's comforting. We've all heard voices in the upstairs hallways, and a few times we've heard what sounds like fiddle music and dancing on the third level. Maybe that could be part of our marketing plan; people would pay extra if they thought they might see a ghost at the B&B. Right?

Julie looked up at a sound from near the piano and gasped. "Dan? Is that you?"

"Sure is, Beloved." Dan smiled that crooked smile of his, his fingers on the keyboard.

The scrapbook slid to the floor as she darted across the room. He rose, meeting her halfway, his hands outstretched. "Are you really here? It's been so long—"

Just before their hands touched, he stepped back, his smile dimming. "I can't stay…"

"Don't leave me! We made a deal, remember? You and I are supposed to grow old together." Julie's voice rose. "I can't raise our kids alone—how can I teach them enough? They need you. *I* need you."

"I can't stay. I love you, Julie, I will love you forever, maybe longer. You're doing great, beloved, raising our girls. They're fine women because of you.

You're teaching them well. You got this. One daughter at a time, remember?"

THE END

If you enjoyed *One Daughter at a Time,* please leave a review on Amazon and Goodreads. Reviews mean more than you know and can even be anonymous. Thanks!

Other Books by Deb Graham

The Ghost in the Bakery
The Dim-Witted Hitman *a cruise crime*
The Cookie Cutter Legacy
Murder on Deck *a cruise novel*
Peril In Paradise *a cruise novel*
Tips From The Cruise Addict's Wife
More Tips From The Cruise Addict's Wife
Mediterranean Cruise With The Cruise Addict's Wife
Alaskan Cruise by the Cruise Addict's Wife
Hand Me That Hand Pie!
The Inspired Writer
Busy Kids, Happy Kids
How To Write Your Story
How To Complain...and get what you deserve
Hungry Kids Campfire Cookbook
On A Stick
Quick and Clever Kids' Crafts
Awesome Science Experiments for Kids
Savory Mug Cooking
Uncommon Household Tips

Bonus chapter from
Peril in Paradise, a cruise novel
by Deb Graham

Jerria's heart beat faster as the limo drew near to the moored ship. Only four years old, the Ocean Haven had already been outclassed by more modern vessels. Carrying only eight hundred six passengers, Jerria and Will had decided it would be just the right size for a journey across the Pacific, disdaining the bigger, newer vessels. Some of those ships hold four thousand passengers; more than double the population of Hat's Mill. Usually frugal, she had asked Will to book a balcony cabin, instead of the ocean-view category they frequently reserved. In Hawaii, the weather would be ideal for sitting out on a balcony. It wasn't too much of a splurge.

The Ocean Haven was to sail at five o'clock. Even though it was not yet noon, passengers with luggage already milled about the pier. Every one of them seemed to be smiling, eagerly anticipating their cruise to Hawaii. A few stragglers from the previous trip waited by the curb for a taxi.

"I love this part, when we see the ship for the first time, Will! Isn't it beautiful? It looks like a big city building. I think our cabin is on the port side. Which one is it, do you suppose? Let's see, deck eight, wasn't it?"

Murmuring unintelligibly, Will smiled. *Good; she doesn't suspect.*

As the stretch limo eased up to the curb, people stared, wondering if there was a celebrity inside. The limo really hadn't cost much more than a taxi. Plus, it made Jerria happy. That was worth a lot to Will.

The limo driver handed their suitcases off to a porter. Tipping them both, Will took Jerria's hand. "Come on, Honey, adventure ahead." Hand in hand, they entered the controlled chaos of the terminal.

Grateful he had remembered to wear his running shoes, Will and Jerria made their way through Security without any problems. His walking shoes had a steel shank in them, and he had set off metal detectors all over Europe during their trip there last year. Glancing at the boarding documents in Will's hand, a smiling agent directed them to a priority line with only three people ahead of them. Will and Jerria were familiar with this cruise line, having taken at least two dozen cruises previously on its other ships.

Craning her head, Jerria frowned, surveying the swarming passengers. "Where is that noise coming from? It must be someone dropping off a passenger, but this is no place for a barking dog. Do you see anything, Will? I think if it was a security animal, it'd be better trained. Besides, they just use those for sniffing luggage, don't they?"

Jerria had a long-standing dislike of dogs; all sizes, all breeds. She couldn't bear their smell, and the fluffy perfumed ones were almost worse. She hated their fur, their glassy eyes, and the way they wiggled and licked, and their tendency to jump on people, especially her. Sensing Jerria's unease, dogs made every effort to win her over. In a room of dog lovers who would welcome nuzzling, they invariably made a beeline to her, begging *'love me love me just give me a chance!'* It was one more reason she enjoyed cruises; pets were not allowed.

As the lines of passengers moved forward, Jerria spotted the offending noise-maker toward the middle of the terminal. While she had great respect for service dogs, the current fad of 'comfort animals' irked her no end, and this was obviously one of those. A real guide dog would be on its own four feet, not in a neon pink carrier with fake gemstones all over the sides. One of those overly fluffy animals, primped within an inch of its life, it had a ridiculous big bow on its head. In another setting, Jerria would've pitied the creature. Surely, even dogs deserve some dignity, and a purpose in life. This one looked like a fancy, frantic fashion accessory.

What kind of an adult carries a live dog around like a teddy bear in a box? Looking closer, Jerria spotted the dog's owner. Appearing to be in her late thirties, the woman could have been much older, under that thick makeup. Or younger; her clothing was certainly too youthful for an adult. On second glance, perhaps she'd borrowed it from her sister, her preteen sister. Exposing the woman's midriff, the white shirt was straining at the seams. To Jerria's practiced eye, there was a real risk of that blouse failing to contain its contents if the woman so much as leaned forward, and there was no way those were God-given attributes. Red satin shorts, as tight as tattoos, and very high heels, bejeweled, of course, completed the look.

The woman's shrill, demanding voice rose over the din. Something about the Disabilities Act. Surely that pampered pet was not a certified service animal! Hearing its owner's high-pitched voice had the unfortunate effect of increasing the dog's volume. Other passengers turned to stare. Was there going to be a full-on scene?

"Honestly, Will, do you hear that? You don't think they'll let her on the ship, do you?"

"Let it go. Even if they do, it's a big ship. Never see her again. Got your passport in hand?"

Anticipating his wife's reaction, Will nudged Jerria forward to the check-in agent's desk, handing over the boarding documents. He'd been careful to keep the freshly printed copies in his own hand, away from his wife's view.

The agent scanned their passports and took their credit card for onboard purchases. "Please excuse me, Mr. and Mrs Danson, while I get your exclusive key cards, and then I will escort you to the VIP lounge where a concierge will show you to your ultra-suite."

As the agent stepped away, Jerria turned to Will. "What is she talking about? We booked a balcony cabin, not a suite. There must be a mix up."

"Surprise, Honey. Upgraded the cabin. Didn't tell you, but the city okayed the purchase of that property down by the river last month. Plan to tear down the old house on it —not safe anymore— and convert it to a city park. Substantial payout." Will caught his wife in a bear hug. "You've been so down lately. Really wanted to surprise you. Want this to be the trip of a lifetime. By the way, an ultra-suite is the best there is. Only five on the ship. Private pool and courtyard. Going to love it."

Before Jerria could protest, the agent was back with the key cards in white envelopes with gold edging. She led them to the terminal's VIP lounge and handed them off to a slim woman in a white dress uniform, obviously a senior staff member.

"Mr. and Mrs Danson, welcome to the Ocean Haven. I am your concierge, Tensa. Follow me, please."

Still stunned, Jerria followed Will and Tensa onto the ship, the familiar bubble of excitement as their key cards slid through the scanner at the top of the gangway magnified. That twangy "bonk" marked the beginning of a vacation. A smiling staff member handed each of them orange juice in a fluted glass. Careful not to get separated from the concierge in the press of passengers, Jerria and Will made their way along the burl wood and brass promenade, through the spacious atrium to a glass elevator. As the elevator rose, Jerria and Will toasted each other.

"I love you, Will, but I can't believe you pulled this off without me knowing."

"So busy making sure Jeff had everything he needed before he left for New York, too distracted to even notice. Last minute deal. Cruise line said they don't usually sell out the ultra-suites. Cost a lot less than you think. This will be our best trip ever, Jerria. Want you to relax and regroup this trip, not think about kids, or home, or worry about anything at all. Ordered our daughters to keep in touch with Jeff. All of them have been freshmen at university, and they know what the boy will need to hear. Off duty, my dear, for the duration of this cruise."

Be sure to leave a review, and pick up the other books by Deb Graham.

Made in the USA
Monee, IL
11 October 2024

66963658R00150